Library of Congress Cataloging-in-Publication Data available.
ISBN 978-1-4521-0795-0

Book design by Eloise Leigh and Mark Neely.
Typeset in Akzidenz-Grotesk Std.

Manufactured in China.

10 9 8 7 6 5 4 3 2

Chronicle Books LLC
680 Second Street, San Francisco, California 94107
www.chroniclekids.com

Visit **www.worstcasescenarios.com** to learn more about the series.

Image credits: Page 189: (tarantula) Johnbell/Dreamstime.com; (river) Johnny Lye/Dreamstime.com; (background) Frenta/Dreamstime.com. Pages 190–191: (background image of South America) NASA Earth Observatory; (woman and child) Courtesy of Emily Caruso; (jungle and river) Guentermanaus/Shutterstock.com; (source of Amazon) Jialiang Gao; (Manaus) King Ho Yim/Dreamstime.com; (house in river) Antonio De Azevedo Negrao/Dreamstime.com. Page 192: (frog) Michal Durinik/Dreamstime.com; (jaguar) Stayer/Shutterstock.com. Page 193: (peccary) Michael Elliot/Dreamstime.com; (anaconda) Morley Read/Dreamstime.com; (caiman) Ammit/Dreamstime.com. Page 194: (mosquito) Mycteria/Dreamstime.com; (tarantula) Luis Louro/Dreamstime.com. Page 195: (wasp nest) Morley Read/Dreamstime.com; (botfly) Yury Maryunin/Dreamstime.com; (tarantula hawk wasp) Paul Nylander. Page 196: King Ho Yim/Dreamstime.com. Page 199: Erllre/Dreamstime.com.

The
WORST-CASE SCENARIO

AN ULTIMATE
ADVENTURE NOVEL

AMAZON

YOU DECIDE HOW TO SURVIVE!

By David Borgenicht and Hena Khan
with Ed Stafford, Amazon consultant

Illustrated by Yancey Labat

chronicle books · san francisco

YOU have been invited to join a one-of-a-kind expedition to the mighty Amazon, the largest river system in the world and home to countless species of plants, animals, and insects. Your mission is to travel by land and water along the entire length of the Amazon River—all the way from its source in the Andes Mountains to its mouth on the coast of Brazil.

As you journey for six months through mountains, hills, and (most of all!) rain forest, you'll be faced with many challenges. The choices you make in each situation will determine what happens to you next. There are twenty-six possible endings to your mission, but only ONE PATH through the book will lead you to the ultimate success.

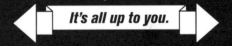

It's all up to you.

How will you know what choices to make? You're armed with your own good judgment and common sense, and you'll have the help of an Expedition File filled with important survival tips. **It starts on page 189—be sure to read it first!**

Get ready to step into an unforgettable adventure in the Amazon, together with a talented team assembled from around the globe. And remember to be careful, because it's a jungle out there!

YOUR EXPEDITION TEAM

STUDENTS

DAN FITZGERALD
AGE: 14
HOME COUNTRY: U.S.A.

An adventurous and fun-loving son of a park ranger, Dan is from Montana and grew up in Yellowstone National Park. He seems to know everything about the great outdoors, and can pitch a tent or tie a knot faster and better than anyone you know. But Dan's most familiar with the North American climate and his knowledge doesn't always apply to the Amazon, even when he thinks it does.

JING YODSUWAN
AGE: 14
HOME COUNTRY: THAILAND

Although she grew up in the crowded city of Bangkok, Jing has spent much of her life trekking through Asia and Central America with her father, an avid hiker and climber. She inherited his passion for the outdoors, and she has a keen eye for details. She is also a skilled amateur photographer. Her quiet nature can be mistaken for shyness, but Jing is actually a very strong leader.

CARLOS MARRA

AGE: 41   HOME COUNTRY: BRAZIL

Your guide is an imposing and inspiring native of Brazil. Carlos led safaris through Tanzania and Kenya for years before returning to his first love, the Amazon, where he's successfully led numerous expeditions. Everything about Carlos is big—his muscular frame, his booming laugh, and his heart. But he expects everyone to give a hundred percent of themselves to his expeditions, and he won't allow anything less.

GUIDE

FREDDY QUISPE

AGE: 27
HOME COUNTRY: PERU

A member of the Ashaninka tribe, Freddy serves as a translator for Spanish and several indigenous dialects. Freddy has two passions in life: languages and soccer, or *fútbol*. He is a team player, and beyond his knack for languages, he understands people and how to keep the peace.

ABADIA MORU

AGE: 32
HOME COUNTRY: BRAZIL

A member of the Ticuna tribe, Abadia is extremely proud of the Amazon's beauty and resources. Her photographic memory and her passion for all living things make her very helpful.

TRANSLATORS

FILMMAKER

NATHAN GREGOR
AGE: 35   HOME COUNTRY: AUSTRALIA

A critically acclaimed documentary filmmaker, Nathan has put himself in extreme situations all over the world to capture amazing footage of wildlife and nature. His fearless spirit leads him to put himself at risk for the perfect shot. His energy is infectious, which means he can often convince others to follow him into danger.

DOCTOR

RANIA SULEIMAN
AGE: 38   HOME COUNTRY: EGYPT

After growing up along the Nile River in Egypt, Rania devoted her medical career to saving lives in disaster zones while working with an international relief organization. She's interested in natural healing and is a vital member of the team. Visiting the Amazon is a lifelong dream of hers, but this expedition is the first of its kind for her.

THE ADVENTURE BEGINS...

APRIL 25, 1:00 P.M.

MT. NEVADO MISMI, PERU

You've just climbed to the top of a snow-capped peak in the Andes Mountains of Peru, and now, near the top, you've found the small spring where the longest river in the world begins. This is the source of the Amazon River! You feel a shiver of excitement as you run your fingers through the ice-cold water.

"Quick, mate, say something brilliant!" says Nathan, his video camera rolling.

"This is absolutely amazing," you say to the camera. "I can't believe it." Even though what you said isn't really brilliant, it's true. It's hard to believe that an unimpressive trickle of a stream on the side of the mountain, marked by a few crosses and plaques, is the beginning of the legendary river.

And it's even harder to believe that you're about to attempt what no kid your age has ever done before: travel the entire length of the Amazon over six months—from the source all the way across the continent of South America to the mouth, where the river empties into the Atlantic Ocean.

Three weeks ago, you started your trek into the Andes Mountains with a team of five others from around the globe. The journey has already been grueling. You've pushed your body through rocky and rough terrain, exerting yourself to the point of exhaustion. You've struggled under the load of a heavy backpack that contains everything you need to survive. And you've battled altitude sickness as your body adjusted to the height of the mountain you're now on.

You and Nathan gaze at the desert-like, mossy landscape around you.

"Not quite the lush green jungle you've always imagined, hey?" Nathan asks.

Nathan, a native Australian who grew up roughing it in the outback, is one of the best nature documentary filmmakers around. His extreme sense of adventure has gotten him into some serious scrapes in the past, but also earned him incredible and award-winning footage from some of the most challenging environments on earth.

You're excited about being part of Nathan's new project. Hopefully, he'll get you on camera doing something more exciting than the everyday things he's been filming so far—like of you setting up camp, eating oatmeal, and even sleeping!

You spot Jing climbing carefully over rocks to reach you. Jing is one of two other students selected for the expedition. She's from Thailand and spent much of her childhood trekking through Asia. At first, you thought Jing was pretty shy, but after three weeks of nothing to do but hike and talk for twelve hours a day, you've learned that she's really friendly and self-confident. Jing is an aspiring photographer, and it's been cool to see the images she captures through her lens—they've shown you things you wouldn't have noticed otherwise.

Between Jing's photos, Nathan's video clips, and your writing, your team is creating a cool interactive website that students at schools around the world will use to track your progress through the Amazon. That's the deal: in exchange for missing a semester of school while you're on a six-month expedition, you have to post a daily journal entry about your experiences. Not bad!

"Carlos wants us to camp here tonight," Jing says to you and Nathan, a little out of breath after catching up to you.

"Okay, let's get Dan. He wandered down that way a little to wash up," Nathan says. Dan, the third student on your mission, is the son of a park ranger and grew up in Montana. He's an experienced climber, a walking encyclopedia of nature-related knowledge, and incredibly handy. Though you were surprised to learn that he's never traveled outside the United States before, so far that hasn't slowed him down a bit.

"Dan!" you call out as you see him sitting by a little stream.

"Hey. This feels great. You guys should join me." Dan's boots are thrown off and his feet are splashing in the water.

"Looks cool, but we have to start making camp now," you say.

"What's for dinner?" Dan, who's always hungry, asks.

"It's Rania's turn to cook. I bet it'll be beans and rice again," Jing says.

During the first week of your trek, you had a lot of different types of food to choose from, but over the past two weeks, as your supply of your favorites dwindled, the team's been limited to what's been left. That's meant a whole lot of beans and rice now.

"Rania's pretty good at spicing things up," Dan replies. "Let's go. I'm starving!"

Rania is in the process of making a fire as the four of you walk back to your campsite. She's a doctor from Egypt, and, lucky for everyone on the trip, she knows her way around a kitchen as well as a hospital. Rania's a gourmet cook and has even taken lessons from famous chefs. Though everyone takes turns preparing the same foods, with the same ingredients, somehow her meals always taste a little better. As you sit around the fire, eating your savory beans and rice and feeling your energy come back, you think about the whirlwind of events that brought you to this place.

It was only six months ago that your science teacher told you about the expedition and encouraged you to check it out. You sent in an application, and six weeks later you were contacted by a program coordinator. You thought you did great in your interview, but you didn't hear anything for a whole month after that. Then one afternoon, you received a call directly from Carlos, the expedition leader.

"I'm impressed with your good judgment, your leadership skills, and your devotion to helping the environment," Carlos said in his Portuguese-accented English. "We could use someone like you on this mission. Are you up for the challenge of the Amazon?" he asked.

"You bet!" you replied, your heart pounding, trying not to shout as you realized that *you* were lucky enough to be selected from thousands of applicants to join this historic mission.

Over six months, you'll journey over 4,000 miles (6,437 km) through Peru, Colombia, and Brazil, by foot, raft, and boat. You'll experience the largest ecosystem on the planet, home to one-fifth of the world's water supply, the largest tropical rain forest in the world, and countless plant and animal species—many of which have yet to be discovered.

After finishing dinner, the team drinks steaming cups of tea sweetened with honey. It feels great to hold the warm cup on the cool mountaintop. This after-dinner tea has become your favorite part of the trek, when everyone sits together and discusses the day's events.

"We've completed an important part of our mission today," Carlos tells the group. "Next we'll head down the mountain and then pass through some mossy, treeless terrain for a few weeks before we finally head into the rain forest."

Carlos, a native Brazilian, has led tons of successful expeditions through Central and South America. He also lived in East Africa for several years, where he was a safari leader. His booming voice intimidates most people the first time they meet him, and that included you. But he quickly puts everyone at ease with his big smile and easy laugh. The only time you have good reason to be scared of Carlos is if you're doing something that puts you or someone else in danger.

"Three cheers for the rain forest!" Nathan shouts. Everyone joins in.

"I've really been impressed with the way everyone's been working together and supporting each other so far," Carlos adds after the cheers die down. "Now let's get some good rest because tomorrow's going to be another long day."

You've become an expert at setting up your tent, so you're in your sleeping bag and fast asleep in no time.

～♐ ～

It's been a month of long days. The first three weeks through the mossy, treeless terrain felt endless. It was hard to keep the entries in your journal interesting, as the days all seemed to blend together into a cycle of hike, camp, repeat. The pattern was interrupted by only a few short stops in small towns, where you got to recharge batteries for the team's laptop, cameras, and other equipment, and replenish your food supplies.

When you felt like you couldn't take another day of walking, the team got to enjoy a week's break, traveling by boat on the lower stretches of the Apurímac River and into the serene River Ene, where the water is calmer and the rapids not as violent as they are upriver. Everyone felt rejuvenated as you feasted on fresh fish, caught on a line off the boat, and enjoyed the water's breeze. Your tired legs had a chance to recover too.

Today, your first day back on foot, you walk a short distance, and then—*wow!* You're startled by the sight of a massive green canopy that extends as far as your eye can see. It's breathtakingly beautiful, with shades of emerald blending together, reflecting the rays of the sun. This is it: you are finally about to enter into the Amazonian rain forest. Then, almost on cue, you hear a loud wail, and a shiver goes up your spine.

"What is THAT?" you ask. "Howler monkeys. Don't be afraid. They won't hurt anyone," says Freddy. He joined your team in the last small town you passed through. When you first met Freddy, a native of the Ashaninka tribe, you weren't sure how to react to him. He was dressed in a *cushma*, a traditional outfit that looked like a giant burlap sack, and he was decorated with feathers and beads. And he had paint on his face, bands around his arms, and a silver pin in his lower lip.

"Do you want to get the camera rolling?" you had whispered nervously to Nathan as Freddy approached your team with a stern expression that made you think you were all in trouble for passing through his village. But the next thing you knew, he was hugging Carlos, and when you were introduced to him, he outstretched his arm and shook your hand warmly.

Freddy speaks several indigenous languages as well as Spanish, and English, of course, and is serving as your team's translator. Plus, he knows this part of the jungle better than anyone, so it's really helpful to have him along.

You're glad to hear that howler monkeys are harmless, because they sound like they could rip your head off. It's a little scary, and you wish they would just be quiet. But, you quickly learn, the rain forest is a noisy place, given the calls and chirps of monkeys, birds, and other animals, the swishing of gigantic leaves, and the humming, buzzing, and clicking of various insects.

Just as your ears have to adjust to the sounds, your body has to adjust to the temperature and humidity of the rain forest. You're sweating a lot, even though you don't realize it, and your shirt constantly feels soggy.

After a day's hike, the team sets up camp in an area that's away from the dangers of flash floods. You've heard horror stories of entire camps being washed away by rising waters at night, and are glad that you have both experts and technology to help guide you. Carlos and Freddy use a global positioning system (GPS) and on-screen maps to determine the safest places to camp. Instead of the tents you used on the high-altitude plains in Peru, you string up hammocks between trees to keep you off the living jungle floor, and that's where you write your blog, under the canopy of your mosquito net.

Apart from a breathtaking variety of critters and plants in the jungle, the heat and humidity, and the hammocks, the other major difference compared to the dry forest is how difficult it can be to pass through all the vegetation. At first, you just tried pushing through with your arms, but you realized quickly that you'd end up with too many cuts and scratches that way. Each of you was given a machete, and as you hike, you often have to cut through enormous leaves and vines to clear a path for yourself.

You're walking through a particularly dense area, slicing through leaves. It's really slow going, and your arms are starting to tire, but it's the only way to make progress.

You see Jing up ahead, and
you try to follow her so you can squeeze
through some of the same areas she clears. But they
close up so quickly, you often have to cut a new path.

You swing your machete—left, right, left, right—and
are walking along when suddenly . . . *whoosh!*

Your blade has cut through a giant bees' nest that was hidden on the underside of an even larger leaf. You see a swarm of angry bees start to emerge, and you do what anyone would do in that instant ... RUN!

You throw the machete on the ground and backtrack the way you came, pushing through the foliage with your body and shouting, "Bees! Bees!"

The swarm is following you, and you're getting stung. *Ouch!* Do you throw off your backpack so you can run faster and swat at the bees with your arms, or do you keep your backpack on and lie down on the forest floor with your hands over your mouth?

IF YOU RUN AND SWAT THE BEES, TURN TO PAGE 53.

IF YOU LIE ON THE FOREST FLOOR, TURN TO PAGE 134.

"Don't touch it!" you shout, as you swat Jing's arm away. The blue frog hops off her backpack and disappears under a bush. "They're really poisonous!"

"Oh my gosh!" Jing gasps. "I wasn't thinking. For some reason, I just really wanted to hold it."

You can understand why. The frog was so cute, like the tiny rubber toys you used to get in goody bags as a little kid, but you know that even a slight touch of their skin on yours can be lethal. And the more brightly colored the frog, the more poisonous it is.

"Let's get back to camp," Jing says. "I've got enough photos for today. And I've had enough close calls!"

"Sure," you say. "It's getting late anyway."

The two of you head back in the direction you came in. Or so you thought. After a while, you realize that you've been walking in a big circle, and you end up in the same spot you were in before.

"I think camp is that way," Jing says, pointing to your left.

"Are you sure? I thought it was that way." You point in the opposite direction.

Uh oh. This could be bad. You do *not* want to be lost in the jungle.

TURN TO PAGE 159.

"Okay. I'm coming," you say. You take the extra battery out of the camera bag that Nathan's left on the shore and walk to the edge of the river.

"It's starting to get dark," you caution again. "Remember, caimans hunt at night."

"Do you see any gators around here?" Nathan asks. "It's clear. And I'll be done filming in a few minutes."

You look at the anaconda and understand why Nathan doesn't want to stop filming. The mammoth snake, which is the largest in the world, is simply astonishing. It could be as long as six of you! You're are amazed that you're lucky enough to see the mighty snake sunning itself on a branch. Anacondas spend a lot of time hidden underwater until their prey come near them. Then they wrap themselves around whatever's unlucky enough to come along—like fish, deer, caimans, and tapirs.

Taking a good look around again, you don't see anything. So you gently wade into the water, carrying the battery high enough that it won't get wet. Caimans are attracted to splashing, so you're careful not to stir up the waters.

"Thanks, mate. See, you're hardly making a ripple and won't disturb a thing," Nathan says.

"This will be amazing to put on the blog tonight," you reply, starting to get excited about the comments that students from all around the world post about your entries. You know that they're learning a lot about the Amazon from you—and it feels great to get fan mail.

Suddenly, you hear Nathan yell. Something is pulling him into the river!

"What the . . ." he shouts, letting go of the camera. PLOP!

Caimans. You knew it! You start to stumble back to shore, but next thing you know, you feel something sharp pierce your foot and yank you underwater . . .

THE END

"If it's okay with you, I think we should keep trying to get back to camp," you say. Even though you could try to build a shelter and wait out the night, you doubt you'd actually be able to get any sleep without your hammock or mosquito net. Plus, you know everyone must be worried sick about you. If you don't come back all night, who knows what kind of panic that might create.

"That's fine," Jing says. "I'm scared of sleeping out here anyway."

You mark the tree where you are and start to walk in one direction, flattening the vegetation on the ground to make a clear path. Then you follow your path back to your tree and make another path outward, looking for signs of the route you took from camp. You do this a few more times, making a new path each time. But as it gets darker, it's getting more and more difficult to make your way without getting hurt.

"Watch out!" Jing says as you stumble over a fallen tree branch in the dark. You feel a thorn scrape along your pants and tear them a little, and you check for blood. You wonder what you and Jing will look like when you finally do get back to camp. *If* you ever get back.

"OW!"

You suddenly feel a stabbing pain in your shoulder and reach for it, but nothing is there.

"What happened?" Jing asks nervously.

You feel your shoulder throbbing and blood flowing.

"Something bit me!" you gasp.

"I saw it fly away," Jing says. "I think it was a vampire bat!"

You hope Jing is wrong. Vampire bats don't suck *all* your blood out like in horror movies, but they bite with razor-like teeth and suck out some of it. And, they can give you rabies in the process.

Jing uses a shirt to help you stop the bleeding and builds a lean-to shelter for you to take cover in for the rest of the night. But you can't sleep, both because of the pain and because you keep imagining what other dangers are lurking in the jungle. In the morning, you have a fierce headache and your shoulder is stiff and swollen.

"Are you going to be able to hike?" Jing asks.

"I'll try," you say, even though you wonder how long you'll last. But after only a few minutes, you hear shouting through the trees.

"Over here!" Jing yells.

Carlos and Dan rush toward you. You've been found! You're in a daze while they start asking you a million questions about what happened. Jing does the talking while you both guzzle water on the way back to camp.

You're relieved to rejoin the rest of the team, and you feel a little better once Rania gives you some medicine for your pain. But, unfortunately, the pain doesn't stop there. You're evacuated to a hospital back home so you can get a series of rabies shots over the next four weeks. *Ouch!* And to make things even worse, everyone you know insists on joking that you must be a vampire now.

Not funny, you think. *Not funny at all.*

THE END

With your fingertips, you try to squeeze out whatever is causing the bump on your arm. But pressing hard on either side of the bump doesn't work: nothing comes out. Using the edge of a fingernail, you dig into it and make the hole bigger. It looks like something is in there, but you can't reach it.

The next day, there's a red ring around the bump, and it's become even more sensitive. You still see something in there, and pick at it again, this time with tweezers. You pull out half of a tiny white worm. The rest breaks off and stays inside you. *Gross!* You show Carlos.

"That looks like part of a botfly larva," he tells you, concerned. "If you had covered it up with tape, it would have suffocated, and then you could have removed it safely. You can't pull a larva out while it's alive without breaking it."

After a week, the pain is worse. The broken larva stuck inside you is causing an infection. Rania says that you'll need to have it surgically removed at a hospital back home. You beg to stay, but there's no *worming* your way out of this—you're going home!

THE END

The next morning when you get up, the flooding is so bad around you that your camp feels like an island. But your team and your things are safe.

"Wow. Good thing you didn't pick that spot," Rania says, pointing to the other site you were considering. "We would have lost half of our gear for sure, and that would have set us back weeks!"

The team is deciding whether to try to build a fire or skip the coffee and eat a cold breakfast when Carlos and Freddy return.

"Hey, everyone. Sorry we got delayed last night. It was suddenly too dark, and we were forced to camp before we made it back here," Carlos says.

"But we have a peace offering," Freddy adds with a grin, holding out a few small packages of cookies. Yum!

After a tasty snack, the team gets ready to head out. You and Dan make your way down to the river to collect the fishing nets.

As you're walking along the riverbank, you have to step over a fallen tree that has spikes all over its bark.

"Be careful of those spikes," Dan warns you. "One nearly went through my boot!"

"Whoa. Look at that!" You point to the water.

SOMETHING LURKS IN THE WATER.

FINALLY!

IT'S AN ELECTRIC EEL!

DAN WANTS A CLOSE-UP VIEW.

AWESOME! I CAN'T BELIEVE HOW HUGE IT IS!

BUT HE'S WAY TOO CLOSE FOR COMFORT.

DON'T TOUCH IT!

"Dan!" you shout. But he doesn't respond.

"Dan! Dan!" you shout again. "Get out of the water!" He's just lying there, facedown, not moving.

You can't believe Dan actually reached out for the electric eel, and that he was so unaware of its power. You know that the shock of a mature electric eel can deliver as much as 1,000 volts of electricity, which is enough to knock out an adult.

Dan could drown if you don't get him out of the water, fast. He's not responding to your shouts, and you assume he's unconscious. Do you jump in after him and pull him out of the water?

The electric eel is still hanging around nearby, looking sinister. Is it possible that the eel used all of its electricity on Dan and now needs time to recharge? If so, you could dive right in. But something makes you hesitate. Could the eel deliver another shock? Should you look for a vine to wrap around Dan's body and pull him out without getting into the water yourself? That will take you longer, though, and every second counts . . .

IF YOU JUMP IN THE WATER, TURN TO PAGE 43.

IF YOU LOOK FOR A VINE, TURN TO PAGE 45.

The piranhas look too threatening to pick up with your hands, so you shake the net out into the bottom of your raft. You plan to use your foot to push the fish into a burlap bag. But the fish start flopping around in the raft, and as you try to get them into the bag, one goes overboard. You turn around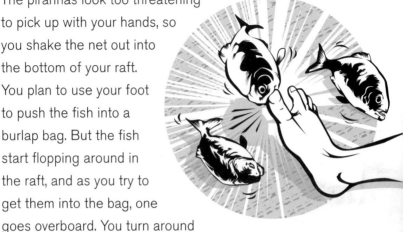
to try to stop another from escaping and . . . OUCH!
A piranha sinks its teeth into your toe! You try to shake it off, but you tip your raft and land in the water with a splash!

"Are you okay?" Jing calls from the shore.

"Yeah, I think so," you gasp, pulling your burlap bag behind you as you climb back onto your raft, empty now of all the piranhas, and paddle to shore. There are only two fish in your bag, and you limp back to camp disappointed to have lost most of your dinner, but also worried about the bite on your toe.

"That looks pretty serious," Jing says, looking at your toe, where a chunk of flesh is missing.

Back at camp, the team makes a stew out of the two fish, while Rania dresses your wound.

"This should heal okay," she says, "as long as you keep it clean and dry."

Unfortunately, in the rain forest, you can't keep the area very clean *or* dry. Over the next week, the bite area gets infected and looks like a giant ulcer. Even though you take antibiotics, you end up getting a raging fever and headache.

"We need to get you to a town with medical facilities where you can recover for a few days," Rania advises.

"A few days? But won't that delay the mission?" you ask.

You see Rania and Carlos exchange a glance, and you realize that the mission will go on as scheduled, only without *you*. And all because of a measly fish, which really *bites*.

THE END

You reach down into the net, grabbing a piranha by the tail. It starts to flop around like crazy. The slippery fish is hard to hold on to, and . . . SPLASH! It flips back into the water. You try to lift another fish, and this time watch the teeth of the piranha come dangerously close to your elbow. You let go of the fish and watch it escape.

You end up losing several fish the same way, until the net slips out of your hand altogether and the rest of the catch swims to freedom. Jing shouts something to you from the shore, but you can't hear what she said until she repeats it when you get closer.

"What did you do? You're supposed to grab them by the gills!"

You see the disappointment on her face and, later, from the rest of the team, when you get back to camp empty-handed. Everyone grumbles as they eat only beans and rice again, and you find yourself imagining what a fresh catch with some garlic and onion would taste like.

That night, when you're looking for a good spot to hang your hammock, you notice some fruit on a tree that you don't recognize. The fruit is ripe and smells sweet. Your mouth waters as you think about how delicious it will be, especially after yet another bland dinner.

You know that there are plenty of foods in the jungle that are unsafe to eat, but this one looks and smells a lot like an apple to you. Do you take a bite, or do you rub a little of the fruit on your skin?

IF YOU TAKE A BITE OF THE FRUIT, TURN TO PAGE 168.

IF YOU RUB SOME OF THE FRUIT ON YOUR SKIN, TURN TO PAGE 95.

You jump into the water and wrap your arms around Dan's body. The electric eel looks right at you, and doesn't move. But then, suddenly . . . ZAP! You feel a jolt go through your body, like you've stuck your finger in an electrical outlet.

The next thing you know, you come to, sputtering and coughing. You must have passed out briefly. You see Dan lying facedown a few feet from you, and you drag his limp body to shore.

"Dan!" you shout as you turn his body over. But Dan doesn't respond.

You were trained in CPR, and furiously go through the motions now, pumping Dan's chest and blowing into his mouth. Finally, you hear him gasp, and you almost cry with relief.

"Are you okay?" you ask. "You touched the electric eel and it knocked you out."

"I'm . . . okay," Dan coughs. "Sorry."

You both lie on the shore until you regain your strength, and then walk back to camp and explain to everyone.

"Dan ingested a lot of water. He's lucky you got him out when you did," Rania says.

"But you took a serious risk going into the water instead of using something to get Dan out. If you had gotten a worse shock and stayed unconscious longer. . ." Carlos adds, his voice trailing off.

You don't want to think about that either.

"I don't know what to say," Dan says before heading off to bed, "except thanks for being there for me . . . again."

The next day, Dan is a little slow on your trek. Then, over the next few days, he gets weaker and starts to cough a lot. Pretty soon, he has a high fever and can hardly walk. Rania says he's developed severe pneumonia from the water ingestion.

"I'm taking Dan with Rania to the nearest town to get medical treatment," Carlos tells the team that night. "I'm not sure if he'll be able to return with us, or what will happen to our mission. I'm leaving you with Freddy for now."

Carlos doesn't ask, but you figure he could use more help getting Dan to town. The part of you that feels responsible for not getting him out of the water quicker—by using a vine to pull him out—is encouraging you to volunteer to go with them. The other part of you feels that you've done enough already and wants to continue on the mission, putting this situation behind you. Dan will be in good hands with or without you. What do you do?

IF YOU HELP GET DAN TO TOWN, TURN TO PAGE 122.

IF YOU CONTINUE WITH FREDDY, TURN TO PAGE 171.

You run over to a tree nearby, cut off a long piece of vine, and tie a loop around one end. Then you throw the loop around Dan's body and use it to pull him toward shore. When he's close enough, you grab hold of him and drag him onto the riverbank. Meanwhile, the eel stares at you and doesn't move. You are about to try to resuscitate Dan when he starts to cough and sputter.

Phew!

"You're okay, Dan," you say.

"What happened?" he asks.

"The electric eel zapped you. Why in the world did you touch it?"

"I didn't think the shock would be so strong," he replies.

Dan's shoulders are shaking, and you realize that he's started to cry.

Oh great.

"I know Carlos is going to kick me off the expedition, after the snake incident and now this. I don't want to leave," he sniffles.

"Look, that's between you and Carlos. Let's go find the others," you say, a little irritated now. Maybe Dan *should* go back home. You have to admit, his poor judgment at times *does* put him and others in danger.

The two of you hurry to catch up with the team, but you leave Dan to tell Carlos what happened on his own.

"You WHAT?" you hear Carlos explode from across the camp. When you get closer, you see that Dan's face is beet red, and he just looks at the ground as Carlos gestures wildly and shouts. It doesn't look good. Later, Dan comes over to you.

"Carlos is furious and said he wants to send me home at the next town we stop in. He says I could have drowned if you weren't with me."

"What are you going to do?" you ask.

"If I have to go home, I have to go home," he responds sadly.

You know he was careless, but looking at Dan's face

and thinking about all the ways he's been helpful on this mission, you realize that you hope he doesn't have to leave.

Another month has passed and you are now in the heart of Brazil. In the end, Dan wasn't sent back to Montana. By the time you reached the next town, Carlos had cooled off and decided to give Dan another chance. And since you all got a nice break boating down the Amazon for two weeks, everyone's been in a great mood.

When you set out to hike again, in a town called Amatura, you all said good-bye to Freddy since he was scheduled to rejoin his family in Peru. You're going to miss his company. The next day you met your new interpreter for the remaining two months of the trip, Abadia. She's a member of the Ticuna tribe, and she speaks English, Portuguese, and some Spanish in addition to her native language. Plus Abadia seems to know everything about the Amazon.

You enjoy spending time with Abadia and are happy to go out and explore with her and Rania one afternoon. Abadia points out a palm tree with large sharp spines all over its trunk. It has a reddish-orange fruit growing in bunches on it.

Abadia slices open one of the fruit, revealing a yellowish flesh and a big seed inside. She offers you a bite, and you expect something sweet, like a peach, especially since it's called a peach palm fruit. But instead it's bland like a potato.

"It's pretty good," you say politely.

"We'll boil these in some salty water for dinner tonight," Abadia says, smiling at your reaction.

As you're walking, your feet start to hurt. Even though you've been trying to care for your feet well, you've developed big blisters. You see a bunch of young Ticuna boys playing barefoot in the river, and you wish you could run and join them. One boy is fishing and you see him pull up a piranha.

Abadia says a few words in Ticuna to the boy. He smiles at her and hands her a fish. She tries to refuse it, but he insists that she take it.

That night, Abadia and Rania cook up a pot of soup with the potato-like fruit and the fish in it. The smell of garlic and onion hangs in the air as you look over photos on Jing's digital camera to post with your blog entry. Your favorites are the close-ups she's taken of a giant water lily, an iguana, a toucan, and a tiny sparrow hawk.

"People need to understand how much we stand to lose if the rain forest isn't protected from destruction and overuse," Abadia says. "You guys are doing a lot to share the riches of the Amazon with the world."

The next morning you go out to collect more of the fruits Abadia showed you. As you walk gingerly, favoring the

foot with the worst blister, you see the friendly Ticuna boy who gave Abadia the fish near the river, and you wave. He smiles and waves back at you. As you continue walking, the boy suddenly shouts, "*Culebra!*" You're not sure what that means, so you slow down.

"*Culebra!*" he says again, this time in a more urgent tone, waving his hands. What is he trying to tell you? Does he need help? Do you hurry toward him, or do you stop?

IF YOU HURRY TOWARD HIM, TURN TO PAGE 183.

IF YOU STOP, TURN TO PAGE 76.

You get into your hammock and are soundly asleep under your mosquito net within minutes. A few hours later, in the early hours of the morning . . .

The sky is falling as your eyes open to a wall of darkness crashing toward you. And then you black out.

The next thing you know, you hear Rania's muffled voice saying, "Can you hear me? Don't move. We're going to get you out." And then there's nothing but blackness again.

You wake up the next day in a cot and see an Ashaninka woman in the corner of the small room. There's a cast on your leg and a bandage wrapped around your head. You feel a dull pain throughout your body and heaviness over your eyes, making them want to stay closed. The woman sees you stir and calls outside. Carlos and Rania rush inside.

"Thank goodness you're awake!" Carlos says. "We were so worried."

"What happened?" you ask. "Where am I?"

"A huge branch of deadwood fell on your hammock while you were sleeping and you were crushed underneath. You're lucky to be alive," Carlos says.

"Your leg is broken in two places and you have some fractured ribs," Rania adds with a concerned expression. "But the scariest part is the major concussion you suffered. You've been in and out of consciousness for the past twenty-four hours. It's too dangerous for you to stay here any longer without proper medical attention. I'm afraid we're going to have to send you home.

Home? Your hopes for making history are crushed along with your hammock. The team has to push forward without you. As they work their way across the Amazon, you will work on walking again.

THE END

You throw off your backpack and swat at the bees with your arms, trying to keep them from stinging your face. The angry swarm seems larger than before, and bees are attacking you from every angle. You are stung everywhere—on your arms, face, neck—even under your clothes.

"Get down!" Carlos shouts. You don't know where to go, so you curl up in a ball and wait for the nightmare to end.

When the bees finally move away, you slowly get up, gather your things, and walk toward the others.

"Bee attack?" Rania gasps when she sees you.

"A bad one," Carlos says and then turns to you. "I was trying to tell you to lie down on the ground and shield your face, especially your mouth. You don't want stings in your mouth."

Rania spends the next hour pulling stingers out of your skin and applying an ointment to your stings, while the rest of the team makes camp early. Later, as you sit by the fire, puffy faced and swollen and in too much pain to even eat, Freddy tries to cheer you up.

"You know, bee stings are part of the jungle experience. We all get stung eventually. Don't let this get you down."

You nod, but even that hurts. You just want to get to sleep, and the antihistamine that Rania gave you is making you drowsy.

The next morning you are still really sore, but the team

has to keep moving to avoid falling behind schedule. You feel guilty for costing the team half a day, so you're determined to push through the pain. As you make your way through the jungle, you check under every leaf before cutting through it. It takes longer, but you shudder at the idea of any more swarms coming after you.

During lunch, you are sitting on a rock when suddenly a gigantic dark-blue wasp with rust-colored wings and a giant stinger lands right next to you. You stay still, hoping it will fly away. But you're holding an empty metal plate and can smash it dead before it stings you or anyone else. Do you do it?

IF YOU STAY STILL, TURN TO PAGE 97.

IF YOU SMASH THE WASP, TURN TO PAGE 124.

You try to outrun the shadow, but it's getting closer and closer to you until ... CRASH! You feel a tremendous whack on your head and fall to the ground. You awake to the crushing pain of a giant branch lying across your chest, pinning you to the ground.

"Help me," you call out weakly. No one responds other than a beetle that crawls across your face.

"Help me ... someone ... please," you repeat.

You hope that Nathan passes you on his way back to camp, provided he didn't get attacked by caimans. Or that a native person comes along and finds you. Or that anyone else—Carlos, Rania, your third-grade physical education teacher, you don't care who—moves the branch off you and makes the pain go away.

You wait and wait and wait, and the pain starts to make you delirious. Finally, you are thrilled to see that a movie starts to play. Nice ... are these home movies? You're confused. Until ... *wait a minute.* You realize that this must be what it's like to watch your life flash before your eyes ...

THE END

YOU FOLLOW THE PECCARY TRACKS.

THIS WAY! LET'S GO!

AND FIND THE PACK.

YOU WAIT FOR THE PIGS TO STOP HOGGING THE FRUIT.

"Let's forget about the peccaries," you say. "They could just cause more trouble, and not lead us anywhere."

"Yeah, I guess so," Jing agrees.

You walk to the banks of the river and dig a hole in the sand. It quickly fills up with water, and the sand acts like a natural filter. Then you take your extra T-shirt and stretch it over the mouth of your water bottle. You use the lid to scoop water out of the hole and into the bottle. The T-shirt strains out any large particles of debris and dirt. It's a slow process, but eventually you fill your bottle with water and then do the same with Jing's.

"Cheers!" you joke, tapping your bottle against Jing's as you both drink nervously. The last thing you want is a water-borne disease or diarrhea in the jungle, but this is the best you can do right now.

You look around for something to eat. After a couple of hours, Jing finds some sour lemons, and you eat them ravenously. And then you spend the rest of the day trying to figure out how to get back to camp.

"Do you think they are still looking for us?" Jing asks when you sit down for a break.

"Of course."

"Do you think they've told our families that we're missing?"

You hope not. You can only imagine what kind of panic that would create.

"Let's not think about it. We'll be found, or we'll find them. And we have access to food and water. We'll be okay." You hope you sound more confident than you feel.

The day drags on and you are no closer to finding camp. You and Jing are exhausted and stressed out at the thought of spending another night in the jungle. But you make it through another uncomfortable night in a lean-to shelter.

The next morning, as you're wandering around, you luckily stumble across a trading post. You have no money, but a kind Ticuna shop owner offers you some hot food and tea. He doesn't speak any English, but when you motion for a telephone, he points you outside, where you find the village's only phone, connected to a satellite dish.

You place a call to the satellite phone Carlos carries for emergencies, and you're so relieved to hear his voice, you almost cry. When Carlos arrives that evening, you're thrilled to be reuinted with the team. But then comes some crushing news. Carlos tells you that he was in touch with your family while you were lost, and when he called to tell them you were found, they insisted that you quit the mission and come home. *Adios!*

THE END

"Hey little guy," Jing says, gently touching the tiny blue frog and pushing it toward her other hand. The frog obediently hops off the backpack and lands exactly where she wants.

"Quick, take the picture!" Jing says. You lean in with her camera, focus the lens, and snap several shots of Jing and the frog. Then you show her the photos.

"That one would be good for the blog," she says, impressed.

Jing takes the camera back, and after a few more photos, you both head back for dinner.

As you're walking, Jing suddenly starts to mumble.

"I'm not feeling so hot," she says.

You look at her face and she's broken into a sweat.

"What's the matter?" you ask.

"I feel . . . dizzy," she says, clutching your arm to keep from falling over.

You see her eyes roll back in her head. She isn't breathing.

"Jing!" you shout. "Breathe!"

Jing collapses on the ground. You lay her flat on her back and try to administer CPR the way you were trained to do before this trip. You compress her chest, counting to ten, and then blow into her mouth. And then you repeat. She still isn't breathing, so you repeat the motions again. Finally, Jing starts to breathe on her own and you tear back to camp.

"Help! Help! Jing passed out!" you shout.

Rania and Freddy run back to Jing with you. You watch as they work on Jing, and nervously answer the questions Rania yells out.

"What did she last eat?" she asks.

"I don't know," you answer. "She was totally fine and having fun taking pictures of a little frog."

"Frog?" Freddy gasps. "Did she touch a poison dart frog?"

You envision the photo of Jing and the frog that you took. *Poison?* Your stomach sinks as you realize that might have been your friend's last shot.

THE END

At the trading post in the next town you stop in, you look longingly at the selection of candy, but you don't pick anything up. Carlos collects some essentials for the group, and you all recharge the team's laptop and camera batteries. As a special treat, the team enjoys a nice lunch—some fried plantains and roasted chicken, complete with homemade chocolate custard for dessert. And things get even better when, after lunch, Carlos tells you that you'll be traveling by boat for the next couple weeks.

"Brilliant!" Nathan says. "I could use a break from hiking."

Boating always puts everyone in a good mood. Apart from rest for your weary legs, you get to enjoy the scenery and feast on fresh fish every day. Pretty soon, you realize that you made a good decision not to lose the rain gear. Even though it's really warm and humid in the rain forest, on the water the wind picks up and you're often wet from waves splashing into the boat. It gets very chilly!

One afternoon, Carlos stops the boat for a while to allow Nathan to get some film footage of massive sloths in the jungle, and asks the rest of you to stretch your legs and look for some fresh fruit on the shore.

"Whoever brings me the most papayas gets a prize!" he teases.

Just the word *papaya* makes your mouth water. The fruit

is quickly becoming one of your favorites, along with guava. When you go back home, you're really going to miss the succulent tropical fruits you enjoy eating ripe off the plant. Even if you find papaya in your local grocery store, you know it won't taste nearly the same after being plucked green, packed in a refrigerator, shipped, and allowed to ripen on the shelf.

As you're walking and looking around, you spot a new kind of fruit on a tree that looks like a green apple. You pull a soft one off the tree, and a sweetness wafts toward your nose. You hear your stomach gurgle. Should you sample the new fruit and see what it tastes like before grabbing more for the team? It seems like the perfect snack, since it's soft and easy to peel. Most unsafe foods are unappealing or hard to get to. Still, would it be better for you to rub a little on your skin to see how it reacts?

IF YOU TAKE A BITE OF THE FRUIT, TURN TO PAGE 168.

IF YOU RUB THE FRUIT ON YOUR SKIN, TURN TO PAGE 95.

"Nathan, I'm sorry but I'm not coming into that water," you say. "And if I were you, I'd get out in a hurry."

"Are you serious? You're going to bail on me?" Nathan scowls. "So much for being a mate."

"Look, I'm just doing what I think is best. I wouldn't take any chances if I were you," you say as you start to back away from the water.

"I haven't gotten to where I am today without taking chances," Nathan yells after you.

You know Nathan is willing to put his life on the line for his award-winning documentaries—and has done it more than once. But as much as you like the idea of making a good film, to you it's simply not worth getting devoured by a pack of hungry caimans. And there's no mistaking that you saw a caiman's nest. Where there's a nest, you figure there must be a mother around. Or a father. Or a whole family. And you are *not* interested in running into any of them.

You feel a little guilty leaving Nathan alone, but you hope he gets out of the water quickly and gets back to camp safely. As you walk, you think about the anaconda and how massive it was. You know those snakes are rarely seen by humans, so it's a big deal that Nathan is getting to film it. And you know that he would love to catch it in action, attacking its prey. Hopefully, he doesn't wait around too long for that to happen.

It's starting to get darker and as you rush along, you take care not to trip over the fallen branches and vines on the jungle floor. You realize that your flashlight is with the other equipment you left behind with Nathan. *Drat.* You pick up the pace so you can be back before it gets too dark for you to see. Besides, your growling stomach is giving you another reason to hurry. Hopefully, Dan hasn't eaten up everything there is for dinner!

CRACK! You hear a thunderous noise and glance around, but you don't see anything. Then, a huge dark mass starts to fall toward you. It's a large branch of a tree, which could crush you if it lands on you. You start to run away from the shadow. But which direction should you go?

IF YOU RUN AWAY FROM THE TREE, TURN TO PAGE 55.

IF YOU RUN SIDEWAYS, TURN TO PAGE 100.

The last thing you want is to be known as the whiner of the group, so you don't tell anyone about your painful feet and push on with the rest of the team, even though the next day you are even more uncomfortable. Every time you take a step, it feels like pins and needles are going through your feet, and you can't help but wince as you walk. After a while, Rania notices and comes up to you.

"What's going on with you? Are you okay?" she asks.

"It's my feet. They've been killing me," you confess.

Rania makes you sit down and take off your boots. As you peel off your socks, she lets out a cry.

"Oh no! This isn't just blisters—it's a terrible infection. I can't believe you didn't say something to me before."

"I didn't want to complain," you say, feeling foolish.

"Well, you should have. You're going to have to take some serious medications and stay off these feet for a couple days while they recover."

Now you feel even worse. You delay the mission by three days, which means the team has to try to make up the time to reach its goal on schedule.

TURN TO PAGE 104.

"I think I should eat this, even though I don't feel like it," you tell Dan. "I haven't had much to eat all day."

Rania overhears you and comes over to where you are.

"That's a good idea. You need the salt to replenish your body, especially in this heat. You've been sweating out a lot of salt. Look!" She points to your T-shirt. "See all that white stuff on your shirt? That's salt coming out of your body."

"Yuck," you say.

"It's totally natural, while your body adjusts to this climate," Rania adds. "After a few days, you won't lose as much. But in the meantime, it's really important to have plenty of salt and liquids so you don't dehydrate."

"Do you think that's why I'm dragging so much today?" you ask.

"It sounds like it *could* be dehydration," Rania says. "I'll mix you an oral rehydration packet to be safe."

You sip the drink and start to feel less queasy. But even though you're feeling a little better physically, you can't help being a little embarrassed about all the fuss over you. First you had the bee stings to deal with, and now maybe dehydration. What's next?

The next day, you make sure you eat all your meals, and even sprinkle some salt on your oatmeal. And you keep drinking, even when you're not thirsty. You notice a huge difference in the amount of energy you have, and during the week ahead, you continue to pay attention to what you eat and drink. The last thing you want to do is slow down the expedition.

One evening several weeks later, Carlos calls you over. You find him standing with Dan, and Carlos sends the two of you to collect firewood together. Even though Dan's been nothing but friendly to you, you've discovered that he keeps to himself a lot. You're glad to have the chance to hang out and talk.

"You know, I'm surprised we haven't had many up-close views of animals so far," he says. "Apart from some bees, that is."

"Very funny," you reply. "You're lucky that you haven't been stung . . . yet."

"I'm serious," he says. "We see some cool birds and monkeys and iguanas here and there. But I want to see some of the other really cool stuff we read about in our expedition file, like electric eels and poison dart frogs!"

"We've only been in the tropical rain forest for a month so far," you say.

"Yeah, but I think we need to poke around a bit more to discover things. I bet you the animals are here and we just aren't noticing them."

"Yeah, maybe," you agree.

"I heard Nathan complaining yesterday that he hasn't filmed anything too exciting yet," Dan continues.

You think back on the past few months. There's been plenty of natural beauty, you've enjoyed meeting the indigenous people, and there have been amazing tropical birds, small mammals, and insects to discover. But Nathan had a close encounter with a herd of angry rhinoceros when he was in Tanzania and a near-death experience involving polar bears in the Arctic . . . so maybe things haven't been as

thrilling to him as they have been to you.

"Let's just grab that pile of wood over there and then go down by the river and see if we can find some electric eels," Dan suggests.

You want to see cool animals as much as Dan does. And you're glad that he wants to explore with you. At the same time, though, you know that the others take their time when they pick firewood, to make sure it's critter-free and dry.

Do you tell him that you think you both should do the same?
Or will that make you seem like a stick-in-the-mud?

Dan reaches for a pile of dead wood lying on the
ground.

"This looks good enough, right?" he asks.

IF YOU SAY, "YEAH! GO FOR IT!" TURN TO PAGE 147.

IF YOU SAY, "NO! WAIT A MINUTE!" TURN TO PAGE 106.

You resist the urge to poke at the bump and cover it with tape instead. You're guessing that the bump is the work of a botfly. Botflies lay eggs on mosquitos, and sometimes when you get bitten by a mosquito, the larva—or baby—of the botfly gets under your skin. As the maggot-like botfly larva burrows into your skin, feeding on you and growing, the bump grows larger and more painful. *Disgusting!*

The botfly larva breathes through the tiny hole at the tip of the bump. By covering the bump with a piece of tape, you cut off the larva's air supply. Eventually the larva will start to come to the surface of your skin for air, and then you can pull or squeeze it out.

You cringe at the idea of a tiny worm living inside you and, if that's not bad enough, eating your flesh! But you try not to think about it for the next couple days. Then you finally ask Rania to see if the larva can be removed yet.

"Yuck. Sorry you have to deal with this nasty critter," Rania says. "But it's a good thing you didn't start poking at it too soon. You could have broken off part of the larva in your body, and that could have caused a serious infection."

"Do you think it'll come out?" you ask.

"Let's see," Rania says.

She cleans her hands with a sterile pad and gently presses on either side of your bump as if she's trying to pop a pimple. *Ouch!* The area is sensitive and it hurts.

"I know it doesn't feel good," Rania says. "But I'm going to see if it comes fully to the surface so I can squeeze it out."

She squeezes a little more. "There it is!"

Rania gently pushes the larva out so it doesn't break inside you. As you see the tiny worm-like critter coming out of your skin, you feel a little queasy.

Finally, the larva is out.

"Ha! I got you!" Rania says triumphantly. She throws the larva away and cleans the small hole it left behind with iodine.

"Good riddance," you say.

"That should heal in no time since the hole is so small," Rania tells you with a comforting pat on the shoulder.

"Thanks," you say, glad that this experience is over.

"What happened?" Jing asks you after you're all cleaned up and bandaged. "Did your little friend come out and say hi yet?"

"Very funny," you reply. "We got it out. Talk about gross!"

"You should have called me over. I could have taken pictures of you two together. Are you going to post about this on your blog?" Jing teases.

Actually, you wonder if you should. How many kids back home have parasites growing inside their bodies? Not many. It might be something they'd want to hear about.

"I'm going to head out to take some pictures. Want to come?" Jing asks.

"Sure." You learn a little more about photography every time you see Jing in action. Plus, sometimes it feels like everyone—including you—is so focused on the goal of getting through the Amazon that you forget to stop and enjoy the wonders of this incredible place. Jing's good at reminding everyone to take a look around.

You and Jing head out together and the creatures of the rain forest are cooperating. Jing spots a brightly colored parrot sitting on a low-lying tree branch, as if it's posing for the camera.

"Check that out!" she says.

Jing takes several pictures. You focus on the trees, wandering around until you find some little monkeys you've never seen before. Jing snaps away, excited. Then, you look up and suddenly spot an enormous toucan with its distinctive curved and colorful beak. *Awesome!*

You're having a great time, but after about an hour, you tell Jing that you think you should return to camp.

"Okay. Let's go," she says, packing up her camera. You walk for a while, but when you get to the campsite, there's no sign of anyone.

"Where did everyone go?" you ask. "Isn't this where camp is?"

"I thought so," Jing replies. "Did they leave us?"

"No, they wouldn't do that. Wait . . . there's no sign of a campfire here."

"Uh oh. Are we . . . lost?"

You hope not. You both try to find the tree where you first spotted the parrot so you can retrace your steps. But all the trees look the same. *Yikes.*

TURN TO PAGE 159.

You stop in your tracks, and then you see what the boy was trying to warn you about: an enormous pit viper is lying on a tree branch not far from your head, poised to strike. You step back from the snake, while the boy comes toward you carrying his machete.

When you are a safe distance away, the boy raises his machete and, using the flat side of the blade, strikes the snake on the head. It is killed instantly, and falls from the tree to the ground, where you stare at it, stunned. The boy says something else to you that you don't understand. All you can say in return is "thank you!" and hope he understands.

Back at camp, you tell everyone what happened. Abadia

repeats the word "*culebra*" and tells everyone that it's a common word for all types of snakes in Spanish.

"He probably thought you'd understand him more than if he warned you in Ticuna."

"But why did the boy kill the snake?" you ask. "It didn't bite me, so he could have just left it alone, right?"

"The snakes are dangerous and territorial," Abadia responds. "It might have bitten the next person after you."

A bite from a pit viper can be deadly—the poisonous venom can lead to organ failure, massive bleeding, and even death. You figure it was better to be safe than sorry.

The next day when you head out from the camp, you look for the Ticuna boy. He's near the same spot again, and he waves at you. You stop and pull out a package of cookies that Freddy gave you, and you offer it to the boy. You wish you had more to offer, but he lights up and takes the package with a smile. Then he runs off to share the cookies with his friends.

That morning, the river has flooded a lot of the area that you and your team are walking through. Every few minutes, you stop to empty out the water from your boots, but the soggy socks you're wearing are aggravating the blisters on your feet. It's slow going, especially because you have to cut through the jungle to clear a path.

FLOODING MAKES FOR SLOW PROGRESS THROUGH THE JUNGLE.

WADING THROUGH THE WATER CAN BE TREACHEROUS.

BE CAREFUL NOT TO STEP ON SPIKES.

YOU CUT THROUGH THE FOLIAGE TO MOVE FORWARD.

You're drenched, and you're covered in mud! The team decides to break for lunch and give you a chance to change and wash out your stuff. Since you're rinsing them in murky water, they're still pretty dirty when you're done.

"I think we should inflate our rafts and use them to float where the water is deeper after lunch," Carlos says. "That might help us move faster so we don't get behind schedule, and make it to our next stop on time."

You're glad that you'll get a break from trudging through the swampy jungle. Your feet are killing you, and every step you take is more painful than the last.

"My feet are really sore," you tell Carlos.

"So are mine," he nods. "Make sure you air them out at night and put powder on them."

As you change your clothes, you examine the blisters on your feet. *Nasty!* Your heels are raw and red and look like someone put them through a cheese grater. You'll powder them tonight, but you wonder if you should show them to Rania too. Maybe she'll have another suggestion? On the other hand, you don't want Carlos to think you're complaining or being a wimp, since everyone's feet hurt.

IF YOU PUSH THROUGH THE PAIN, TURN TO PAGE 66.

IF YOU SHOW RANIA YOUR FEET, TURN TO PAGE 126.

"Here you go, Dan," you say, handing him your plate. "I'm going to bed."

You drag yourself over to your hammock, feeling a little light-headed, and you fall asleep.

The next morning, you feel even worse. You have a brain-splitting headache and are extremely nauseated. You can't even get out of your hammock. Jing comes over to see you.

"You okay?" she asks.

"I don't feel good," you moan.

The next thing you know, Rania is by your side, taking your temperature and checking your pulse.

"Your heart is racing and you have a fever. What was the last thing you ate?" she asks you.

"I wasn't hungry yesterday," you mumble.

A few minutes later, Rania brings you a bottle and orders you to sit up. "You are seriously dehydrated. Sip this slowly."

She hands you the bottle, filled with oral rehydration solution, and you taste it. *Bleh.*

"Doesn't matter if you don't like it," you hear Carlos say. "Drink it."

You feel like a little kid being forced to take medicine, but you obediently drink it, trying hard not to throw up.

"You've been sweating a lot but not feeling it because of the extreme humidity," Carlos explains. "Even if you're not thirsty, you have to keep drinking."

"And it's just as important to eat," Rania adds. "Why do you think we put so much salt in the beans? We're sweating out so much salt that the body needs."

"Look!" Carlos points to his shirt, where there are white stains. "That's salt. When you adjust to the climate, you won't lose as much."

Luckily, by drinking the solution, you feel the nausea start to pass. By evening, your fever is down and your headache is almost gone. The bad news is that you've delayed the trek by an entire day.

TURN TO PAGE 104.

You head over to where Freddy is sitting by the campfire repairing small holes in the fishing nets.

"Can we chat for a minute?" you ask.

"Sure, what's going on?"

"Dan, Jing, and I couldn't agree what to do about the peccaries. Jing wanted to scare them, but Dan thought we should run. So he did. And now Jing's pretty upset that Dan left us," you explain.

"What about you?"

"I don't know. I'm not mad at Dan. But I kind of feel stuck in the middle."

Freddy nods sympathetically. "I've been on a lot of expeditions. And sometimes relationships between team members are even harder to navigate than the jungle," he says with a laugh.

"What should I do?" you ask.

"Well, everyone is going to disagree at times. That's natural. I think the best thing you can do is try to get Dan and Jing to talk it out."

That makes sense to you. You decide to talk to them both in the morning.

"*Gracias,* Freddy," you say, feeling a little better.

"*De nada!*" he smiles.

The next morning Carlos announces that because

of the river flooding, the team has to change course. Now, instead of passing through the town you were supposed to go through today, you'll be heading around it.

Meanwhile, Freddy is going to take Carlos on a short detour to a small village he knows of, where they'll stock up on some essential food supplies.

"We'll move faster if it's just the two of us. And that way we won't lose a day. We'll meet back up with the rest of you at the coordinates we give you," Carlos explains.

"Right, mate, no problem," Nathan says. "We'll be fine."

Before they leave, Carlos and Freddy give you and the others some of the load from their backpacks so they won't be weighed down. You struggle a bit with the extra weight. Luckily, you don't have too far to travel today.

"Listen, Jing," you say as you fall into line next to her. "I don't think we should be mad at Dan for what happened yesterday. That moment was scary for all of us, and he was just doing what he thought was right."

"He could have trusted me," Jing says. "I was the one who was right after all. It was in our Expedition File!"

"Well, I think he realizes that now. I can tell that he feels embarrassed about what happened, and he got hurt. Let's just put this behind us."

Jing continues to walk, stopping to take a picture of

a beautiful flower. She doesn't respond, but her expression softens, and you know she's thinking over what you said.

Later you help Dan cut through some branches.

"Look, I'm really sorry about not listening to you guys yesterday. I should have stuck with you, even if I thought you were wrong," he says.

"Don't worry about it. You had a right to do what you thought was best."

"Thanks, but I think Jing is really upset with me," he continues.

"You should just talk to her about it," you suggest. "You guys are friends, and this shouldn't get in the way."

Dan heads over to where Jing is, and you see them talking and—after a few minutes—laughing together. Freddy was right, and you're glad that you could help smooth things over between them.

The team arrives at the coordinates where Freddy and Carlos asked you to meet, but there's no sign of them yet. They usually determine where to set up camp, but it's getting late and you're all tired and hungry. You're relieved that you didn't use up the battery left on your handheld computer last night, so you can now find a safe spot to camp. With the river flooding, you can't be too careful. You study the maps on the screen. Which site do you choose?

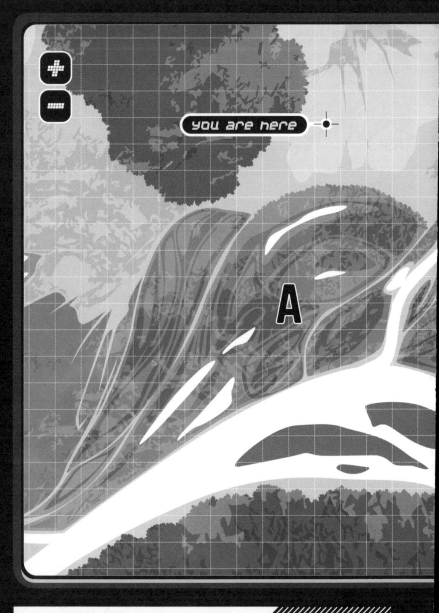

you are here

A

IF YOU CHOOSE SITE A, TURN TO PAGE 140.

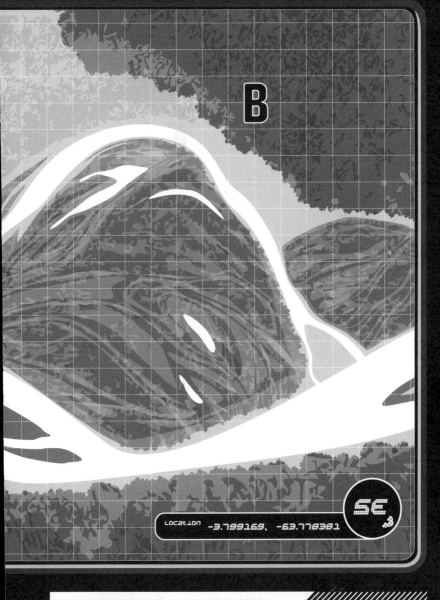

LOCATION -3.799169, -63.778381

IF YOU CHOOSE SITE B, TURN TO PAGE 35.

"No, Dan. You can't take chances with something like this. Stay here and try not to move too much. In case you did get bitten by a poisonous snake, you don't want the venom to spread in your body or get to your heart. I'll be right back!"

You tear back to camp as quickly as you can, and luckily you find Rania there, reading a book. As you breathlessly tell her what happened, she grabs the anti-venom medication and races after you back to Dan. When you get to him, Dan's

eyes are closed and his face is very white. You start to panic.

"Stay calm," Rania says, "I need your help. Dan must be in a terrible amount of pain now, and the toxins can shut down his body's systems if we aren't fast enough. Just take a deep breath and roll up his sleeve while I mix the anti-venom compound."

After what feels like forever, but is actually only a few seconds, she injects the medicine into Dan's arm.

"Now let's just hope that we made it to him in time," Rania says. As she speaks, Carlos approaches.

"What's going on? I saw the two of you run out of camp like there was a fire or something," he says.

You fill Carlos in about how Dan didn't want you to get help right away.

"It's good you didn't listen to him," Carlos says. "That was a coral snake you described. He's really unlucky to have been bitten by one, but lucky that you were there. He could have died."

"Am I going to be okay?" You turn and see that Dan's eyes are now open.

"I think so," Rania says. "Let's get you back to camp."

The rest of the team crowds around Dan when you return, wanting to know what happened.

"Bad luck, mate!" Nathan says.

"Poor Dan," Jing adds.

Rania sets up a schedule where each of you takes turns watching Dan during the night, to make sure he doesn't have any trouble breathing or any other serious problems. In the morning, he looks better, and the anti-venom medication seems to have worked. Rania is much more relaxed than the day before, and even starts to joke around with Dan a little to try to make him smile.

Carlos and Rania decide to let Dan recover for another day before continuing on your trek. "We'll just try to make up the lost time later," Carlos says. You see his furrowed forehead, and you can tell he's tense about being able to keep you all safe. This was a close call.

You and Jing decide to spend your free day exploring in the jungle and taking photographs. As you walk along, a small nut lands at your feet, and you look up to see a little monkey in the tree above you.

"Look, Jing! He's so cute! Take a picture of him."

Jing pulls her camera out of her backpack and moves closer to get a better look. The monkey throws a nut at her, too. You pick it up and throw it gently back, but the monkey runs away in the tree.

The next thing you know, the monkey returns with two friends, and all *three* of them start throwing nuts at you and

Jing. You laugh and try to dodge them. Who knew you could play a game with a bunch of monkeys!

Jing gets some great close-ups and action shots of the monkeys.

"This will be great for the blog!" she says.

You look around for other cool animals to photograph and spot a few tropical birds unlike any you've ever seen before. Jing finds interesting leaves and insects to shoot too. When it's time to head back to camp, Jing realizes she's left her backpack over where the monkeys were. You walk back to collect it, and when Jing gets close, she stops.

"How cute! Look at the tiny blue frog sitting on my backpack! I love frogs! Will you get a picture of me holding it?

She reaches down to pick it up. Do you stop her?

IF YOU STOP HER, TURN TO PAGE 28.

IF YOU LET HER CONTINUE, TURN TO PAGE 60.

"These guys look serious," you say in a low voice to Jing. "I don't want to mess with them. It's not worth it—we have a mission to finish."

"I agree," Jing adds. "Let's get out of here!"

You look at Freddy and motion that you are leaving. He nods at you and then turns his attention back to the angry men.

You and Jing slip away while the others are still trying to communicate, and getting louder. You jog until you feel you're a safe distance away.

"What now?" Jing pants.

"I think we should head back to the nearest town. We'll try to call Carlos and see what he wants us to do."

"Won't he get upset at us for splitting up?"

"Yeah, probably. But we have to try to let him know what's happening. And besides, either we get this mission going again, or we're going home."

Jing looks distressed. "We can't stop now! So many people are counting on us."

Jing's right. You don't want to think about how many people will be disappointed if you go home, including you!

Suddenly, you see Jing's eyes grow wide. Now what?

Jaguar! A big cat has come out of the trees and is staring at you. You look at its large, muscular body and feel sheer terror at the thought of it lunging at you.

"It sees us!" Jing whispers.

"What should we do?" you ask.

"On the count of three, let's run," Jing says.

You haven't done anything to provoke the cat. Maybe if you get out of its way, it'll leave you alone. Or you could try to intimidate it by raising your arms, standing tall, and staring it down. If it knows you mean business, it might back down too.

IF YOU RUN FROM THE JAGUAR, TURN TO PAGE 174.

IF YOU TRY TO INTIMIDATE THE JAGUAR, TURN TO PAGE 158.

You take the fruit and rub its skin and a piece of its flesh back and forth on your arm. Then you wait to see what happens. If the fruit is poisonous, or causes an allergic reaction, you'll know it's not safe to eat. Sure enough, after about fifteen minutes, you see a small rash break out on your arm. Better not to eat this, whatever it is!

Back at camp, you describe the fruit to Rania.

"That sounds like the fruit of the *strychnos* plant, which has a poisonous bark that people have been using for a long time for arrows and recently for medicinal purposes," she says. "I'm not sure if the fruit of the plant is poisonous, but it's not worth eating, even if it just disagrees with you."

"Yeah, I guess so." You imagine that a case of diarrhea would be extra unpleasant in the jungle.

"I know everyone is tired of eating the same food all the time. How about if I make us some savory pan bread tonight? And I think Freddy still has some dried papayas. We can make some kind of dessert out of them."

"Thanks!" Rania is always looking out for you. She's got a warm and nurturing personality that's really comforting. You're sure she is a really nice doctor to all of her patients.

"No problem. Just promise to stick to fruit and berries that you recognize or that someone else identifies as safe to eat," she adds.

"Deal!"

After a satisfying dinner of Rania's pan bread, three-bean-and-potato stew, and dried fruit pudding, you volunteer to take the dishes down to the river to  rinse them out. You're sitting on a big rock in the water near the shore, watching crumbs float away, when you turn to reach for the frying pan.

Eek! On a rock between you and the bank sits an enormous tarantula, the size of a large dinner plate! Its dark hairy body injects sudden fear into you, paralyzing you for a second, even though it hasn't touched you . . . for now. You'll have to step on that rock, scary spider and all, to get back to land.

You look behind you and the water in the river is high and flowing pretty fast. Do you avoid the rock and swim a little bit downstream to get away from the tarantula? Or do you go ahead and step on the rock where the tarantula sits?

IF YOU JUMP INTO THE RIVER, TURN TO PAGE 150.

IF YOU STEP ON THE ROCK WITH THE TARANTULA, TURN TO PAGE 102.

Even though you're tempted to swat at the wasp with your plate, you take a look at its giant stinger and slowly move away from it instead. Tarantula hawk wasps *look* really threatening and their supersized stingers pack in extra pain, but unless you provoke them, they'll leave you alone.

You think about what Freddy said about relaxing about the bees, and you know he's right. You're going to have to get over what happened and not freak out. If you had hit that wasp, you'd probably be howling in pain right now. You take a deep breath, and decide that even if you get stung again during this expedition, you'll handle it. Plus, now you know how to better protect yourself.

"How are you feeling, mate?" Nathan asks you as you walk over to where he's checking the battery levels of his camera.

"A lot better than yesterday," you say.

"Are you up to joining me on a filming session? I could use another pair of hands."

"Sure," you reply. Nathan is always a lot of fun. Plus, you could use some of the video clips for your blog and going with him will help you get ideas for what to write about.

You head toward the river together and don't find anything extraordinary for a long time, until . . .

BUT YOU SEE SOMETHING ELSE THAT SIGNALS DANGER.

THAT'S A CAIMAN NEST. THEY'RE ACTIVE AFTER DARK. LET'S GET OUT OF HERE!

NATHAN ISN'T AFRAID, AND HE ISN'T GOING ANYWHERE.

I'M NOT STIRRING UP THE WATER, AND I DON'T SEE ANY CROCS. CAN YOU BRING ME THAT EXTRA BATTERY PACK?

ARE YOU GOING TO HELP HIM OUT?

IF YOU JOIN NATHAN IN THE WATER, TURN TO PAGE 29.

IF YOU DON'T, TURN TO PAGE 64.

You run sideways, avoiding the shadow of the falling tree. Your lungs are hurting and you pant from running so fast, but it's worth it. You hear an enormous thud, as a gigantic branch falls behind you, narrowly missing you.

You wonder what might have happened if you were crushed by the tree. It could have broken some bones, caused a concussion, or worse. You shudder, thinking about all the dangers of this wild but beautiful rain forest. There's a reason so few people have done what your team is doing.

When you get back to camp, you tell Carlos what happened with Nathan.

"I don't want to sound like a tattletale," you start. "But I didn't feel comfortable staying around the river where there was a caiman nest, and it was starting to get dark. So I left."

"I understand," Carlos says. "I'm glad you told me. And even though I wish Nathan had come back with you, you did the right thing."

You tell the others about the anaconda.

"Awesome!" Dan says. "What was it doing?"

"It was lying on a branch along the river, and it yawned a few times. I think Nathan really wanted something exciting to happen, so he was waiting around for that."

"The snake must not have been in a hunting mood," Freddy chimes in. "If it was hunting, you guys probably wouldn't have seen it. Anacondas hide their entire bodies under water with nothing but their nostrils sticking out for long stretches. They just wait there for their prey to come along."

Next you describe your narrow escape from a falling tree, and everyone agrees that you've had an eventful day. But after an hour passes and Nathan still hasn't returned, Carlos approaches you.

"Can you take me back to the part of the river where you guys were earlier? I'm getting worried."

"No problem," you say, hoping nothing terrible has happened to Nathan.

When you reach the river, you witness a distressing and bloody scene. Nathan is lying on the banks. His clothes are in shreds and part of his arm has been chewed off. *Caiman!* Semi-conscious, Nathan stirs and moves his lips when he sees you.

"Don't speak," Carlos says. "We're going to get you out of here and get you help."

Nathan is evacuated to Manaus by helicopter. After he is stable, he is sent back to Australia so doctors can save what's left of his arm. Without him filming the expedition, a big *chunk* of your sponsorship money dries up. The mission is cut off.

THE END

Even though it looks really scary, bringing back fears from horror movies and Halloween, you remind yourself that tarantulas have a worse reputation than they deserve. Even though they eat all sorts of insects and, in some cases, even tiny birds, tarantulas are not harmful to humans. Their bites are actually no worse than bee stings. Even still, you've had your share of bites and don't want any more. You quietly pick up the pots and pans, keeping an eye on the tarantula. And then you step on the rock, putting your foot right next to it. It doesn't move. Phew!

On the way back to camp, you pass a bunch of guava trees and spot some nice-looking fruits hanging just out of reach. After your failed luck with the other fruit, it would be nice to come back to camp with a bunch of these. And, out of all the tropical fruits you've tasted, guavas are your favorite.

You leave the dishes at the base of the tree and hoist yourself onto a low-lying branch. *Easy!* Then you climb up a little more until you're well off the ground, to where the biggest and juiciest fruits are hidden.

Your pockets are filled in no time. And then you pause and sink your teeth into a guava. *Yum!* You see a large, super-ripe fruit on a branch above you and reach for it. As you move your arm . . . WHOA! You lose your footing and almost fall out of the tree. You grab onto a branch and regain your balance, breathing heavily until . . . CRACK! The branch you are standing on snaps, and you tumble out of the tree.

You land with a thud on the ground and feel a jolt of pain going through your hip and leg. *OW!* Waiting for a minute for the pain to pass doesn't help. You try to stand and almost faint. But you have no other option but to drag yourself back to camp, limping and dragging your leg behind you.

"What happened to you?" Jing gasps when she sees you. She runs up to you and yells for Rania.

"You most likely broke your leg," Rania says with a grimace. "You need to get to a hospital. Immediately."

Looks like you're going home. You can't get through the jungle on crutches. You try to savor your last Amazonian guava, but somehow it doesn't taste very sweet at all.

THE END

The last few days have left you feeling worse than you've felt in a long time, and you wonder when you'll get back to normal. Still, you try your best not to slow the team down any more than you have already. You're feeling self-conscious about being a drag on the mission. And even though no one has said anything to you about it, you can't help but wonder what your teammates are thinking.

As you're hiking, Jing slows down until you catch up to her. "Are you feeling better?" she asks with a friendly smile.

"I'm okay," you say, glad that she doesn't seem frustrated by your slowness.

"Do you want some help carrying your things?" she offers.

Your pack seems heavier than ever, and you were just wishing you could throw it off and leave it behind. In addition to the essential items you need, like your hammock, food, clothes, raft, and laptop computer, you have to carry some stuff that you hardly ever use. It's annoying to have to lug so much around, including things you save for those "rainy day" moments.

"Thanks for offering, but I've got it," you say. You know that Jing's pack is already heavy enough without you adding to it.

But as you walk along, you start to think of other ways

to lighten your load. Is there anything you don't use that you could get rid of? What if you dump your rain jacket? You're wet all the time anyway, and it's been way too hot to wear it. What's the point of keeping it? At the next town you stop in, you could try to sell it or trade it for some candy. Your mouth starts to water as you imagine biting into a chocolate bar, or some fruit chews. It's been so long since you've tasted anything like that—granola bars and nuts just aren't cutting it anymore.

When you arrive at the town, you show a shopkeeper your rain jacket, and he's ready to trade it for some items in his store. You eye the candy and see that you could make the exchange for three different types, and get enough to enjoy for a few days. But what if you need the jacket later? Should you keep it just in case?

IF YOU DECIDE TO TRADE THE RAIN GEAR FOR THE CANDY, TURN TO PAGE 156.

IF YOU DECIDE TO KEEP THE RAIN GEAR, TURN TO PAGE 62.

You and Dan back away from a long snake with red, yellow, and black bands. You're pretty sure it was a coral snake, which is venomous. Luckily, it slides away, not paying either of you any attention.

"Wow! Thank you for doing that," Dan says, shaking his head as he realizes what just happened.

"No problem," you say.

"I should have known better. I was in a hurry and wasn't thinking."

"Well, I guess you'll never forget to 'kick before you pick' again," you say lightly, referring to the warning you read in your Expedition File.

"I'm sure I would have been bitten," Dan continues. If Dan *had* been bitten, he would have been in serious danger. Rania carries anti-venom medication for all of you, but who knows how quickly she could have gotten it to him . . . and if it would have fully done the trick. You don't even want to think about the consequences of that scenario.

"Don't worry about it right now. Just remember for next time," you say.

"No, seriously, if that was a venomous snake, you could have just saved my life. I owe you," Dan says, his voice shaky.

"We all have to look out for each other," you say, feeling a little overwhelmed too. "Come on, let's go get this wood back to camp. Then we can go explore."

"Okay," Dan agrees, still in a daze. You both return to camp in silence.

Back at camp, Dan tells Carlos what happened, and your cheerful expedition leader shows his rare stern side.

"You *what*? That wasn't smart of you, Dan," Carlos scolds. "You're lucky you had someone with you who acted smart. I hope it wasn't a big mistake to bring you on this expedition."

Yikes. That was harsh. You're glad it wasn't you.

"No, no! I promise I'll be more careful," Dan says.

Neither of you are in the mood to explore anymore, so you help with dinner and then sit around the fire. Freddy tells the group about various snake encounters he's had in his life.

"Have you ever seen the world's biggest and heaviest snake?" Nathan asks.

"An anaconda? Yes," Freddy says. "More than once."

"I've actually *eaten* a snake," Dan brags. "A rattlesnake."

"What did it taste like?" you ask.

"Snake meat is really bland," Dan says. "You need lots of hot sauce to make it taste like something."

The thought of eating snake meat—with or without hot sauce—makes you cringe. You hope you won't find snake being cooked on the campfire one night.

You also hope you won't have any more close encounters

with snakes on this trip, but that's very unlikely. Carlos has just warned you all again to be on the lookout for snakes on the ground and in tree branches. And he wasn't just talking about coral snakes. Pit vipers, boa constrictors, and a bunch of other serious snakes make their home in the Amazon.

It's almost nightfall when it's time to hang your hammock, and you want to get under your mosquito net quickly, since the bugs are starting to bite ferociously. Jing already looks very comfortable in her hammock. *Lucky her*, you think.

You look for a good spot to hang your hammock and see two options. Which one should you choose?

IF YOU CHOOSE SITE A, TURN TO PAGE 51.

IF YOU CHOOSE SITE B, TURN TO PAGE 151.

SITE A, THE VIEW LOOKING UP

SITE B, THE VIEW LOOKING UP

"Okay, Dan," you give in. "But let's hurry."

You give another kick to the pile of wood, and nothing else comes out, so you pick up a few dry branches.

After about ten minutes, you see Dan is struggling to stay upright. His face is white and he doesn't look like himself.

"Dan? Are you feeling okay?" you ask.

"I can't breathe," he replies with a gasp.

Dan needs medical attention—and fast. You run back to camp as quickly as you can and shout for Rania.

"Dan was bit by a snake! Hurry!"

Rania grabs her medical bag, which has the anti-venom compound in it. You race back to Dan with Rania right behind.

"We need to get this into Dan's body before the toxins shut down his central nervous system. Every second counts."

As you help Rania administer the medication, you see Dan's eyes roll back in his head.

"I think we may be too late," Rania says. "We need to get Dan out of here, now!"

If Dan dies, your mission will definitely be over. You and Rania each take one of Dan's arms, but as you carry him through the forest, you soon realize that he's not with you anymore . . .

THE END

"Do you think this is the right move?" Jing asks you in a hushed voice. "Shouldn't we be trying to get to town so we can get in touch with Carlos?"

"I don't know," you reply. "I thought you agreed with them?"

"Well I did," Jing says cautiously. "But I also don't want to miss Carlos. And I really want to know how Dan is doing."

"Me too. I'm sure he's much better now and that they're all on their way back to meet us."

Jing doesn't look so confident. But she doesn't say anything else.

You continue to hike through the jungle, following the path that Freddy takes you on. Freddy's skills are really impressive. Now that Carlos isn't around to help him, you see how much Freddy relies on his own knowledge of the rain forest and so little on technology. It's like he has a built-in sense of where he is and where he's going.

Your hike is going smoothly until . . . you're abruptly stopped by three angry-looking tribesmen in native dress holding bows and arrows. They're speaking a language that Freddy doesn't understand, and they point to you, Jing, and Nathan, and frown. Others are watching you. Suddenly a woman behind them sees you and starts screaming and running away.

Nathan steps closer to the men, holding up his hands.

"Easy now," he says.

You can't take your eyes off the arrows, and you hope Nathan stays calm.

By the men's gestures, you understand that they're saying you can't cross through their land. You've heard about tribes who've had bad experiences with foreigners taking advantage of them, grabbing their land, or hurting the rain forest. Some tribes even have myths about foreigners doing terrible things to indigenous people, like peeling off their faces. Maybe that's why that woman seemed so scared of you. You don't blame her. You'd be scared of a face-peeler too!

Nathan is trying to speak in some kind of sign language. You're not sure what he's trying to say as he points to his watch.

One of the tribesmen holds out his hand.

"Um, I think he wants the watch," you tell Nathan.

"Yeah," Jing adds. "Maybe if you give it to him, he'll let us pass."

"My grandfather's watch?" Nathan snorts. "No way!"

"Should we give them something else?" Jing asks.

You start to pull off your backpack to look for something to offer the men, but that only seems to make them even more upset, so you stop.

"What's going on, Freddy?" you ask.

"They want us to leave," he says. *Obviously.*

"Let's just go," urges Jing.

"No," says Nathan. "Let's try to reason with them a little."

"Are you sure we shouldn't leave now?" you ask.

"Listen, you two can go if you want, but I'm not going to be intimidated by these guys."

Nathan isn't backing down. Freddy is standing next to him, looking tough.

You want to get away, but you don't know if you should leave without the whole group. Should you ask Jing to go with you to the nearest town and wait for Carlos? But Freddy is supposed to be in charge of you. Should you wait and see what happens, so you all stay together?

IF YOU LEAVE WITH JING, TURN TO PAGE 93.

IF YOU STAY, TURN TO PAGE 143.

You carefully remove all of the piranhas from the net one by one, without getting bitten once, after grabbing them firmly from behind the gills, and toss them into a basket Jing is holding. The two of you proudly walk back to camp with a harvest of eleven good-sized fish.

"Hurray!" Nathan cheers as you triumphantly dump out the fish in front of everyone.

"Now that's what I'm talking about!" says Carlos. "You managed to harvest piranhas without getting bitten—good job!"

Freddy steps in and quickly has all the fish gutted, de-scaled, and ready to cook. Dan starts a roaring fire to cook them over. In no time, the fish are simmering in a pot, and you watch as Rania whips up a pan bread to go with them.

With a little garlic, salt, and some lemon squeezed on top, the piranha make a five-star meal, and afterward everyone sits back with full bellies, satisfied and happy. Freddy teaches the group an Ashaninka song, and you all clap and sing together.

"Thanks to both of you for your excellent fishing," Carlos says to you and Jing, as you enjoy the merriment and look forward to blogging about the experience. "You didn't just fill our stomachs tonight. You helped boost the mood of the team, and that means a lot."

"You're welcome," you say, glad to have helped. And since you still have some time before it gets dark, you and Jing decide to look for some fruit for dessert. Dan joins you.

"That was a great meal, guys!" he says.

"How was your search for animals with Nathan?" you ask.

"Pretty awesome! We saw some woolly monkeys, which are huge and have these really thick, long tails. And, even better, we saw some black caimans in the river up close."

"Did the black caimans look like regular alligators?" you ask.

"Kind of, but they were enormous! Nathan was lucky enough to film one caiman attacking an iguana. The caiman just lay still in the water and then pounced on the iguana before it knew what was coming, and dragged it underwater," Dan continues.

You've heard that a black caiman can grow to be as long as a car and that caimans eat both small and large animals. Although they don't often attack humans, you don't want to get close enough to tempt any.

"That sounds intense," you say.

"Yeah. I was hoping we'd find some electric eels, but that was pretty awesome," Dan says.

"Look!" Jing interrupts, pointing to the ground. You see some markings in the mud.

"What is that?" you ask.

"Peccary tracks," she says. "Freddy pointed them out to me the other day. And he said that peccaries love fruit. If we follow the tracks, we might find a fruit tree."

Peccaries are large pig-like animals that travel in herds of up to a hundred. They are known to be pretty smelly and have sharp tusks that they use to dig up roots.

Jing senses your hesitation. "Don't worry. These tracks are old. Follow me."

The three of you walk along looking up at the trees for hanging fruit. Sure enough, after a while you find a papaya tree. Around the base of the tree are some ripe papayas that have fallen. You pick up a couple and check to make sure they aren't overripe, or that they haven't been half-eaten by bugs or animals already. And you're happy to see that there is some low-lying fruit that you can pull off the branches of the tree if Dan gives you a boost.

As you're filling your backpack with as much papaya as will fit inside, you hear a faint rumbling sound.

"Is that thunder?" you ask.

The rumbling starts to get louder and soon you can hear a clacking noise. Jing's eyes grow wide.

"I think those are peccaries!" she says. "Freddy thought he heard some in the distance when I was walking with him the other day, and he made a loud whooping sound. I think it scared them away. Let's make a lot of noise too."

"No way! That'll just let the peccaries know exactly where they can find us," Dan protests. "I think we should stay quiet and run for it. And if we need to, we can find a tree to climb."

"I really think we should try to scare them away, Dan," Jing argues.

"But pigs can't climb trees, right?" Dan fires back. "And do you really think they'll be scared by our shouting?"

The rumbling is getting louder. The herd is getting closer.

"Come on guys, quick! We have to do something," you say.

"Let's get out of here!" Dan says.

"No," Jing says, looking at you.

You look back and forth at Jing and Dan. They can't agree on what to do, so it looks like the decision falls on you. Think fast!

IF YOU DECIDE YOU SHOULD RUN, TURN TO PAGE 169.

IF YOU DECIDE YOU SHOULD MAKE LOUD NOISES, TURN TO PAGE 144.

You go find Nathan, and he interviews the logger with Freddy translating, and he gets a lot of detailed information.

"Good idea, mate," Nathan says, thanking you later. "I'm glad we came this way."

"So you're not angry about the El Dorado thing?" you ask.

"Nah. Sure, I was disappointed at first, but it was the right call to stay on course. And look at all this great footage!"

"Great," you say, relieved.

"We're shedding light on a huge issue," Nathan says. "I think people will respond."

You hope so. Your team gets to town and connects with Carlos. Dan's doing better, but his parents freaked out when they heard how sick he was and are taking him home. Jing's parents decided to be cautious, too, when they heard about Dan, so she's going back to Bangkok.

"With both of them out, our sponsorship money will dry up," Carlos tells you, looking glum. "You can arange to go home now, or stick around and help us finish up this documentary for a few weeks. Either way, we're not going to finish this mission."

You decide to stay and help with the documentary. But you also promise yourself that the mission *will* be completed. By *you,* someday, somehow . . .

THE END

"I'll go with you," you volunteer.

Carlos looks at you with a grateful expression. "Are you sure? You may not be able to complete the mission if you come with us."

"I know," you say, trying to ignore the pit in your stomach. But looking at Dan, this feels like the right thing to do.

You, Carlos, Rania, and Dan set out toward the nearest town, which is at least a full day's hike. Carlos wants to get there before nightfall, so you don't have to camp. Dan tries his best to keep up, but you each have to take turns carrying his pack and giving him an arm to lean on. After a few hours of hiking, with frequent stops for rest and water, Dan is panting and wheezing heavily. Rania checks his temperature and looks concerned.

"Dan's overexerting himself. We need to slow down before he has more serious breathing problems."

"No, we've got to push forward in order to get to town before dark," Carlos says with a frown.

"Well, let's break for lunch and see how Dan does with an hour's rest," Rania replies.

While the others are preparing lunch and tending to Dan, you get an idea. You search for a few strong branches and start to bind them together with vines. Before long, you've assembled a basic stretcher that can be used to carry Dan.

"Hey guys, do you think this will help?" you ask, dragging the stretcher behind you.

"Absolutely! That's a great idea," Carlos says. "Dan, would you be okay with us carrying you?"

"Sure," Dan wheezes. "Thanks."

It's difficult to carry Dan, but two of you at a time take turns, and now you move faster than before. And, best of all, Dan's breathing slowly starts to improve.

Finally, after what seems like forever, you approach the town. There isn't much that can be done for Dan medically here, so you'll have to wait for him to be evacuated. Meanwhile, the rest of your team continues to make its way toward the end of the Amazon River basin without you. You fight back tears, trying not to think about what you're missing.

But soon the media hears about the turn of events. You are hailed as a hero for your quick thinking in helping Dan, and you're praised for sacrificing your personal dreams for your teammate. Even better, you're invited on two new expeditions for next year . . . one that will cross the Pacific Ocean and one that's a safari in Africa. Which will you choose?

THE END

You take a swing at the wasp and . . . miss! You quickly try again and swat at it as it flies up toward you. Then you watch in horror as its enormous stinger pokes you in the shoulder. Yow! This sting is extremely painful—worse than all the others. For about three minutes, you are in sheer agony and can do nothing but howl.

Later, Dan reminds you that tarantula hawk wasps aren't even aggressive, unless you're aggressive first.

"If you had just left it alone, it would have left you alone, too," he says, shaking his head sympathetically.

"That's great," you mutter.

"Seriously, you need to relax about the bugs," Dan says. "Or you'll make yourself crazy."

"Well, why don't *you* get attacked first and then talk to me?" you snap back, irritated by Dan's friendly advice.

"I'm just saying," Dan mutters and walks away.

You feel a little bad for losing it, but the bugs *are* making you crazy. Apart from the bees and wasps, you are constantly getting bitten by mosquitoes, and it feels like your entire body is coated with bumps and welts. You can't sleep at night because you're sore or scratching, and it's made you more than a little grumpy.

After a while in the jungle, your body will get used to the mosquitoes, to the point where your skin won't even react. But you're not there yet, and you're so sick of the itchy feeling on your skin. So you keep spraying yourself with insect repellent.

"Whoa! Someone's got a lot of bug spray on," Nathan laughs as he walks by.

You wonder if it even works, because after a couple days, you notice a new raised bump on your arm that doesn't itch like a mosquito bite. It just hurts. Did you get *another* kind of bite? You watch it for a few days, and it doesn't go away. There's a tiny hole at the top of the bump, kind of like a pimple. Could it be a botfly larva living under your skin? You hope not. You feel like squeezing the bump to make whatever is in there come out. Or, you could cover it up with a piece of waterproof tape and see if that helps.

IF YOU TRY TO SQUEEZE OUT THE BUMP, TURN TO PAGE 34.

IF YOU COVER IT UP WITH A PIECE OF TAPE, TURN TO PAGE 72.

"Hey Rania, do you mind taking a quick look at my feet?" you ask quietly, so the others don't hear.

"Of course not. That's what I'm here for," the doctor says. "What's the matter?"

"Well, they've been hurting like crazy, and they look pretty gross," you explain.

Rania examines your feet with a serious expression. Carlos walks up to see what's happening.

"This is really bad!" Rania says. "I can't believe you waited so long to say something."

"Yeah," Carlos agrees. "That's way worse than blisters."

"What's the matter?" you ask.

"Your feet are badly infected. I'm going to give you an ointment and some antibiotics. Hopefully that'll prevent you from getting complications that could prevent you from continuing," Rania says.

You're glad you weren't making a big deal about nothing. The ointment is soothing and you put on the driest socks you can find, although you know they won't stay dry for long.

The team has to keep moving through the flooded forest today, using rafts when the water is deeper and walking when it's shallower. You've been traveling for over four months already and are still on track to make it to the mouth of the Amazon on time, provided there are no more setbacks.

Late in the day, Rania walks along slowly with you. Soon you're both trailing pretty far behind the others. Rania tells you stories of some of the disaster relief camps she's worked in around the world.

"So why'd you decide to come on this expedition, instead of going on another relief mission?" you ask.

"Well," she says, "I've got some sponsors who are funding this trip. If I successfully complete the mission, they'll donate a large sum to the charity group I work for."

"That's awesome." You're impressed by her commitment to helping people.

"Plus, I've always wanted to visit the Amazon, ever since I was a little girl in Egypt living on the Nile. There was always a debate over which of the two rivers was the longest, and only recently was it officially declared to be the Amazon. I had to see this great river for myself!"

You hear a rustling in the foliage and look up, alarmed. It's only Dan, coming back to check on you both.

"You scared me!" you tell him, punching him lightly on the arm.

Then suddenly, you hear the slightest sound behind you and turn around.

You are face-to-face with a jaguar! It's staring right at you, with bright yellow eyes. Your heart races as you

remember Abadia telling you the word *jaguar* comes from the native word *yaguar*, which means "he who kills in a single leap." You can see that this jaguar is poised to pounce.

"Don't run!" Dan says in a loud whisper. "Try to stare it down and intimidate it."

Wait a second. Now Dan's telling you *not* to run? With the peccaries he had said *to* run. What should you do? Do you run? Or do you listen to Dan and stand tall?

IF YOU RUN, TURN TO PAGE 174.

IF YOU STAND TALL, TURN TO PAGE 161.

"Come on, mate," Nathan says. "This could be our destiny!"

"Completing this mission *is* my destiny," you say. "We've come so far, and I don't want to go home with nothing."

"But what about going home with a fortune?" Nathan's eyes light up when he says the word *fortune*, and it's hard not to get drawn in by his enthusiasm. You see Jing nodding, but you resist.

"El Dorado is a myth, Nathan," you say gently. "No one's found it for more than five hundred years. You heard Freddy."

"I heard him say that he believes in the lost city. Besides, Freddy's family goes back for generations. They might have information about the lost city of gold that no one else has."

"But then why haven't they already found it?" you argue.

"Maybe because it's meant for us!" Nathan says.

Nathan's trying every angle to convince you to join him. Freddy is already in. And Jing looks she's ready to go too. But if you refuse to go, the group has no choice but to stick to the original mission. No one's crazy enough to tell Carlos they left you *alone* while they went on a wild good chase.

"I don't want to do it, Nathan," you say. "We should stick to our mission."

"Fine. Forget about it," Nathan says abruptly. But something in his tone makes you think he's not going to forget about this for a while.

"Okay. Now that that's decided, we'll make our way along the river for the next few days," Freddy announces, looking disappointed. "If we're fast, we can reach the spot we were scheduled to get to before Dan had to be taken away."

"What about meeting up with the others?" Jing asks.

"I hope we'll hear from Carlos when we get there," Freddy says.

That sounds like the right plan, and you feel good about your decision. But over the next couple days, you feel awkward, especially around Nathan, even though you try to be friendly. You notice that he seems extra chummy toward Jing, as the two of them talk away about photography and film. Freddy sometimes joins in the conversation, but when you say something, it seems like everyone just gets quiet. You feel unwelcome. And you can't help but blame Nathan for it.

You're also out of ideas for your blog. When you sit down to write at the end of the day, all you can think about is how unreasonable it is for Nathan to make you feel bad about the whole El Dorado situation, and about how angry you are at him. But you don't want to write about that. So you end up just skipping your blog for a couple days.

During your morning hike the next day, the team enters into an area of the rain forest where most of the trees have been cut away. There's nothing but stumps left for as far as

you can see. And it's eerily quiet. Nathan pulls out his camera and starts filming.

"What happened here?" Jing gasps.

"This looks like the work of loggers," Freddy says with a frown. "Sometimes they don't do a good job of carefully selecting which trees to cut down and which to leave. Instead, they just come in and clear out huge parts of the forest."

"Why would they do that? It destroys habitats and messes up the entire ecosystem!" Jing shakes her head.

"Well, it's faster, and there's a lot of money to be made in logging," Freddy explains. "Companies don't think about the long-term damage they're doing to our planet."

You feel a rush of anger toward the loggers who are destroying the precious rain forest. How greedy!

Later that night, you walk with Freddy to the river to wash your clothes. You see a man there rinsing out dishes, and Freddy starts to speak to him in Spanish. You can follow enough of the conversation to understand that this man is a logger.

"Ask him why he would do such a terrible thing," you say.

Freddy poses the question, and the man gives him a long answer with a sad expression.

"He says that he wishes he didn't have to cut down the trees, but that it's the only way he can provide for his family," Freddy translates. "He knows it's harmful, but there aren't many other ways to make a living here. Plus, everyone wants wood. Think about all the things that are made with wood."

You realize that the problem isn't the individual loggers, but the companies that are hiring them, and the people all over the world who are buying stuff from those companies, like fancy dining room tables and hardwood flooring. The story is a lot more complicated than it seems.

Speaking of stories, you wonder if you should write about your encounter with this man in your next blog entry. This could be the story you were looking for. Or, you could suggest to Nathan that he interview the logger on film for his Amazon documentary. It would add a lot to hear what he has to say. The problem is that Nathan has been so chilly toward you recently that he might not like to hear your ideas right now. You can imagine him coming up with a reason why it wouldn't work or just brushing you off.

IF YOU SUGGEST THE INTERVIEW, TURN TO PAGE 121.

IF YOU DON'T SUGGEST IT, TURN TO PAGE 141.

YOU CAN'T SHAKE THE BEES OFF YOUR TRAIL.

YOU DIVE ONTO THE GROUND TO TRY TO PROTECT YOURSELF.

YOU SHIELD YOUR NECK AND MOUTH WITH YOUR HANDS.
SOME BEES STILL MANAGE TO STING YOU.
OUCH!

You've never been stung by more than one bee at a time before now, and, wow, does it hurt! You lie as still as you can until the bees lose interest in you, and then slowly crawl out from the vines.

Carlos and Rania hurry over to where you are.

"You okay? That looked like a nasty swarm," Rania says.

"Yeah," you reply weakly.

"You did the right thing to take cover and protect yourself," Carlos says. "It could have been a lot worse if you were running around."

You shudder at the idea of the swarm attacking you from *all* angles. Luckily, since you had your backpack on and were lying on your front, you were mostly stung on the arms.

"Let me take a look at your stings," Rania says. "We need to get these stingers out and clean the sting area."

Rania applies some ointment to the stings and gives you some antihistamine to help you with the allergic reaction. The team decides to make camp early for your sake.

That night, around the campfire, you're a bit puffy and groggy from the medicine and stings, and feeling generally miserable.

"Hey, want to play a game of checkers?" Dan offers.

"I got some really nice shots of some parrots today. Do you want to see them?" Jing asks.

You're grateful that everyone is trying to cheer you up. But you don't feel like doing anything, and even skip your journal writing. Another dinner of beans and rice isn't appetizing, and you don't eat much. You're swatting at mosquitoes, and it hurts to move your arms. Carlos senses your mood and sits by you to give you a pep talk.

"For better or worse, insects are a natural part of the rain forest. We're all going to get stung and bitten during this expedition—some days more than others. But it's something we just have to push through. Don't worry, kid, you'll feel much better in the morning."

With the aid of the medicine, a good night's sleep *does* help. You're in much better spirits when you wake up the next morning. But you still don't have much of an appetite, and just take a few bites of your oatmeal.

It's another long and strenuous day of hiking. You push through with your machete, slower than usual as you take extra care not to disturb any bees. Freddy is walking alongside you, entertaining you with stories of growing up in the Amazon, and tells you about his love for soccer, or *fútbol.* You can't tell which he's more proud of—the Ashaninka community, or the Peruvian national soccer team—as he rattles off facts about both. Today he's replaced his *cushma* with a bright red-and-white soccer jersey and long shorts.

As entertaining as Freddy is, after a few hours you start to feel super-exhausted. You've drained your water bottle and don't even feel like refilling it from a stream and adding a purifying tablet. You just want to lie down. You're extremely relieved when it's time to camp for the night, and ask Dan for some help stringing up your hammock.

"You feeling alright?" Dan says, concerned. "You don't look so well."

"Yeah, I'm just really tired," you reply.

"Maybe you're hungry. I don't know about you, but I'm starving," Dan says. "I think we have some pan bread to go with our beans tonight. And Jing found some sweet lemons."

"I can't think of eating another bean right now. Any way we could order a pizza?" you joke.

"Oh yeah! Pizza . . . ," Dan says dreamily. "That *would* hit the spot. But I'll eat just about anything right now."

It's time for dinner, and everyone is sitting around with their meal. You look at the mound of salty beans on your plate and push them around with your spoon. You haven't had much food all day, but this is completely unappealing, and you can't bring yourself to eat it. You nibble on a piece of pan bread and suck on half a sweet lemon, which is the best thing you've tasted in a while.

"What's up? Don't like my cooking?" Nathan asks you,

as he notices that you haven't made a dent in the food on your plate.

"No, no. It's fine," you say. "I'm just not hungry."

"I'll eat yours if you don't want it," Dan volunteers.

You know you should probably eat a little more, but the sight of the food is making your stomach turn, and all you want to do is get into your hammock and sleep. Do you force yourself to eat, or do you give your food to Dan?

IF YOU FORCE YOURSELF TO EAT, TURN TO PAGE 67.

IF YOU GIVE DAN YOUR FOOD, TURN TO PAGE 81.

"Oh no!"

You wake the next morning to Jing's cries. From your hammock, you see her standing waist deep in water.

"Look! We weren't on high enough ground! Half of our camp was washed away because of flash floods."

The rest of the team wakes up and, over the next couple hours, there's a lot of commotion and yelling as team members try to chase down items that are caught on tree branches and floating away. But it's hopeless. Too much of your essential equipment has disappeared, and with it, any chances of completing your mission have washed away too.

THE END

You don't say anything to Nathan, but instead you write a long blog entry that night about the logger, the trees, and the companies that are causing the deforestation. The next morning, you ask Jing for some of her photos to upload with your blog.

"Of course," Jing says. "Take a look at those and choose the ones you like best. Can I read your entry?"

"Sure," you say, handing her your computer.

As Jing is reading, Nathan walks up.

"This is really good," Jing says. "That guy had a lot of interesting things to say."

"What guy?" Nathan asks.

"I met a logger yesterday by the river and he was talking to Freddy and me about his work."

"Really? What did he say about the government's role?"

"Um, I didn't ask," you say.

"I wish I could have spoken to him!" Nathan looks disappointed.

"I was thinking of asking you if you wanted to do an interview, but . . ." you don't know how to finish the sentence.

"Wait a second. You thought of it, but you *didn't* ask me? Why in the world not? Do you know what great footage that would have made?"

You stay silent.

"I can't believe it. What a missed opportunity." Nathan shakes his head and looks disgusted. He walks away and you realize that even if Nathan wasn't upset at you before, he certainly is now.

Later, you see Nathan and Freddy talking in the distance. You can't tell if Nathan is chewing out Freddy for not getting him to talk to the logger, or if he's complaining about you. But you see Freddy nod in your direction and you wonder what he's saying.

"I made a mess of things," you tell Jing.

"It's okay," she says. "Everyone makes mistakes."

Freddy comes up to you and Jing. "Nathan wants to find some more loggers to interview. We're going to look around."

But after a couple hours, they come back without finding anything but some guava fruit.

"I need to spend today looking for anyone connected to this logging," Nathan says as you're all eating the fruit. "It's my job to document the deforestation. Is that okay?"

The others agree, and even though you want to push forward to town, you stay quiet. You don't want Nathan to be even more upset with you. Everyone packs up and walks out of the deforested area, back into the jungle, away from your destination.

TURN TO PAGE 113.

You study the tribesmen. It's not fair that they aren't letting you pass through. You're just there to explore, not to hurt anyone.

"Nathan, how about offering them some of our medicines? Do you think they might want them?" you whisper.

"I guess that's worth trying," Nathan replies. Then he turns to the men.

"We have something for you," he says, speaking in a loud voice, as if that will help them understand.

Slowly, you slide off your backpack. As you reach into it, one of the men shouts at the others. *They think you're going for a weapon!* The next thing you know, several arrows are pointed at your face . . .

THE END

"Sorry, Dan," you say. "I think we should try to scare the peccaries away. If Jing thinks that's what worked when Freddy did it, we should try it. He would know best."

"No, I'm the one who's sorry. I'm not going to stand around and get gored by a bunch of smelly pigs!" And just like that, Dan runs away, leaving you and Jing standing there alone.

Jing looks at you and nods slowly. "Let's do this, okay? On a count of three, be as loud as you can be. One. Two. Three. . . ."

The two of you let out the craziest yells you can muster up, whooping and hollering and screaming for about thirty seconds. Your lungs are bursting with the effort of making all that noise.

And then you stop and listen. You still hear the thundering sound of the peccaries' hooves, but it seems to be farther away now, like when a storm is passing.

"I think it worked!" you say.

"Me too," Jing replies, flopping down on the ground, exhausted. "Thanks for backing me up."

"It seemed like the right thing to do. But I hope Dan got back to camp okay."

"Yeah. Although I can't believe he just ditched us and took off." Jing's tone is bitter.

"He just didn't want to take any chances," you say.

"I guess so."

You and Jing walk back to camp and find Dan sitting on a rock, with a big bandage around one leg. He looks up as you approach, and you see a mixture of relief and embarrassment on his face.

"You guys okay?" he asks.

"We made it back in one piece, didn't we?" Jing says curtly, and walks by.

You're not sure what to say or do, so you give Dan a shrug and head back to the fire. You hand Carlos and Rania the papayas from your backpack.

Freddy sees your expression and asks you what's wrong.

"We heard what we thought was a pack of peccaries, and we weren't sure what to do. Jing said you make loud noises to scare them away, so we tried that. And it worked."

"She was right. That was a good thing to do. Peccaries can be really dangerous and you could have been seriously injured," Freddy says.

You look over at Dan, who is too far away to have heard Freddy. Freddy notices your glance.

"Dan fell while running back to camp and got a nasty cut. He's lucky he didn't get hurt worse, or caught by the peccaries" he says. "Do you want to talk about what happened?"

You appreciate the concern, but you don't feel comfortable saying anything more just now. Plus, you're drained.

After setting up your hammock and mosquito net, you take a few minutes to write your journal entry for the day, highlighting the fishing but skipping over the peccaries. As you write, and imagine your friends and family reading your entry, a wave of homesickness comes over you. It's been a week since you've spoken to anyone back home, and you'd really like to hear a familiar voice.

You notice that the computer's battery is getting low, but you have enough power to have a ten-minute conversation with your best friend. You'll be reaching a town tomorrow where you can recharge the batteries. Do you take a few minutes to call your friend to cheer yourself up? Or do you take Freddy up on his offer to chat?

IF YOU DECIDE TO TALK TO FREDDY, TURN TO PAGE 83.

IF YOU DECIDE TO CALL HOME, TURN TO PAGE 173.

"Yeah! Go for it!" you say.

Dan quickly picks up a branch from the pile of wood on the ground and then, even quicker, drops it with a shout. You see a red-, yellow-, and black-banded snake slither away.

"OW! It bit me!" Dan holds up his hand. You can see where the snake's fangs pierced the skin on his finger.

"Oh my gosh! Are you okay?"

"Yeah, yeah, I'm fine," Dan quickly replies. His ears turn red and he looks embarrassed. "I should have known to 'kick and pick.' I wouldn't have been bitten if I had remembered the rule," he adds.

"That's okay," you say. "Everyone makes mistakes . . . and I didn't remind you."

"Man! I don't want to get in trouble for being careless. I need Carlos to trust me on this expedition." Dan shakes his head. His face is red, and you know he is in pain.

"Look, that doesn't matter now. I'll run and get Rania. That could have been a coral snake." Coral snakes are highly venomous. If Dan's been bitten by one, that would be very bad news.

"No, no I don't think so," Dan says quickly. "It was just a milk snake."

"What's a milk snake? Do they even live in the Amazon?"

"They're all over the place. They aren't poisonous, even though they look a lot like coral snakes. Trust me, I saw them all the time in Montana."

"But don't you want to get Rania to look at your hand anyway?" you ask again.

"Yeah, but I'll show her when we're back at camp. It doesn't hurt too badly. Let's just get the firewood like we were supposed to." Dan winces as he speaks.

Snakes are a serious danger in the Amazon—serious enough that Rania carries anti-venom medication for all of you. In addition to coral snakes, you're supposed to be on the lookout for pit vipers, too, as they're also venomous.

Before the expedition, you were clearly instructed by Carlos to "kick before you pick" up anything off the forest floor. Dan's right to be embarrassed at having forgotten.

"But Dan, what if it *was* a coral snake? You don't want to take chances," you say again. How can he be so sure it's *not* a coral snake? You're positive that you clearly saw the colors of the snake: red, yellow, and black in repeated bands.

"Listen. It wasn't," Dan says. "I don't want everyone to freak out."

You aren't sure what to do. Should you run back to camp and get Rania, even though Dan doesn't want you to, or do you let Dan decide for himself what to do?

IF YOU DECIDE TO RUN BACK TO GET RANIA, TURN TO PAGE 88.

IF YOU DECIDE TO LET DAN TAKE CARE OF HIMSELF, TURN TO PAGE 112.

You take another look at the tarantula's hairy body and the last thing you want is to be anywhere near it! Ditching the dishes and deciding to come back for them later, you quickly dive into the river. *Brrrr!* The water is much colder than you expected. You start to swim, but the current is fighting against you. You're paddling furiously with your arms, but you're feeling like you aren't going anywhere. You try to get back to shore and keep getting pulled away.

Whack!

A big rock stops you from going farther, but also gives you a concussion. You fall back into the water and are washed away . . .

WHACK!

THE END

You notice that one of the trees has a lot of dead branches in its canopy. The last thing you need is a branch to fall on you while you're sleeping. So you string up your hammock between two trees with nothing suspicious in their canopies.

You wake up early to the sound of an extremely loud bird calling over your head. It's shrieking, and you try to shoo it away from under your mosquito net. But it doesn't pay you any attention and continues to make its strange sound. Even though you've grown accustomed to the noises of the nocturnal animals, and can mostly sleep through all the howls, croaks, and squawks, this one is too close by and too unfamiliar to tune out.

There's no going back to sleep, so you decide to start on breakfast. Nathan is already up and brewing a pot of strong coffee.

"Good morning, mate! Did you wake up from that racket too?" Nathan asks.

"Yeah. I don't know what kind of bird that was, but it was loud!" you reply.

"No, I meant the sound of that big branch coming down."

Whoa! You look over and see that there's a huge dead branch lying under the tree you didn't choose for your hammock. You would have surely been crushed by the branch if you had been under that tree.

"So I was talking to Carlos last night," Nathan continues, not noticing your changed expression as you quietly thank your lucky stars that you picked the right site for your hammock. "And he thinks we should set up some nets and fish today. Everyone is really tired of eating rice and beans."

"You can say that again," says Jing, coming up to join you.

"If we get a good harvest of fish, we can have a feast tonight," Nathan says, "which we all deserve. And if we have extra, we can dry some out to take with us when we travel inland."

Fish jerky? You wonder what that would taste like; not too fishy you hope.

"Sounds good," you say. "Should we set up the nets now?"

"Sure, we might as well get an early start," Nathan says. "Let me just grab my camera."

Jing joins the two of you on your walk down to the river. With Jing's help, you tie the end of the nets to a rock on the banks. Then you inflate a raft and get in, holding the nets. You paddle yourself out a little bit away from the banks, and set up your nets. Nathan films you the whole time.

Since you have to stay close to collect the fish from the nets later, your team is not going to be hiking today. Everyone is glad for a day of rest and relaxation after weeks of being on the go. Nathan and Dan decide to spend their day in search of

more wildlife. Rania is collecting samples of medicinal plants. And Carlos and Freddy are studying maps and planning your route to make sure you stay on track to finish within the three months you have left.

That leaves you and Jing free to chat while you wait for the fish to fill the nets, and you stretch out luxuriously along the banks of the river.

"I never liked to eat fish growing up in Thailand," Jing tells you. "I remember it used to frustrate my father so much, since he loves to cook seafood. He's so happy to hear that I've been eating just about anything on this trip."

"You don't really have much of a choice. I didn't realize how hard it would be to eat the same food every day, even though they warned us," you confess.

"Me too. It's also hard not having good snacks. I really miss chips and cookies," Jing says. "Although the tropical fruits have been nice."

Your mouth starts to water as you think about the last delicious piece of fruit you had in the jungle— a ripe guava. The apple-shaped fruit with round edible seeds inside was sour and sweet at the same time. It wasn't like any fruit you'd tasted before. You have to admit, for all your complaints about the food, the tropical fruits, when you've found them, have been amazing.

"All this talk of food is making me really hungry," you say. "Let's check the nets. If we collect the fish now, we can clean them and have them ready for dinner."

You give the string of the nets a gentle tug and feel some weight inside. Bingo! You paddle your way out to the nets in the raft again and slowly pull the nets up. You're startled by what you see inside: a big bunch of . . . piranhas!

You feel a little nervous looking at the dark and angry-looking fish with their razor-sharp teeth. They freak you out a bit, since you know they are flesh-eaters. And you want to make sure that *you* make a meal out of *them,* rather than the other way around.

As the piranhas flop about in your net, you wonder how you're going to get them out of the net, without them taking a chunk out of your fingers.

Should you dump out the net into the bottom of the raft, so you can scoop the piranhas into a bag? Or should you reach in? If so, how?

IF YOU REACH INTO THE NET AND PICK UP A PIRANHA BY THE TAIL, TURN TO PAGE 41.

IF YOU REACH INTO THE NET AND PICK UP A PIRANHA FROM BEHIND THE GILLS, TURN TO PAGE 116.

IF YOU DUMP THE NET INTO THE RAFT SO YOU CAN SCOOP UP THE PIRANHAS, TURN TO PAGE 39.

You make the trade and feel satisfied it's a good one. The shopkeeper looks pleased with the rain gear, and you're happy to see it go. You gladly reach for the bag of candy—this is weight you don't mind carrying around for a little while, until it all disappears.

"Look what I got," you show Jing. "Want some?"

"Yum! Sure," Jing says. Dan walks over, and you hand them both pieces of chocolate with caramel inside. It melts in your mouths, and you can't help but giggle as you lick your fingers and point at the chocolate on each other's faces.

"Where'd you get this?" Dan asks.

"I traded it for my rain gear," you say proudly.

"What?" Jing and Dan say together. "You sure that was such a smart idea?" Dan adds.

"We haven't used it in over a month, and it's just getting warmer," you reply. "I'm tired of carrying it around, and this way someone else gets to use it . . . and we get some treats!"

"Well, I hope you don't end up needing it," Jing says in a cautious tone.

Over the next few days, you're more energized, and can't help but think it's from the chocolate. You're in a better mood, too, and you feel a little bounce coming back into your step.

Things continue to look better when you learn that the team is going to be traveling by boat for the next two weeks, making some serious progress down the Amazon in an area that is too difficult to trek through by foot.

Being on a boat is always a welcome break for everyone, and even more so for you this time, since you can use the rest more than ever. Dan catches some fresh fish, which Rania cooks up for the group.

And then it starts to storm. Not a light, passing tropical shower, but a serious dumping. Soon, you're wet, cold, and miserable as you realize this is precisely the moment when you *needed* your rain gear. Carlos asks you where yours is, and you have to confess that you traded it for candy. The look on his face is one you'll never forget.

Even worse, since you're still a little weaker than normal, you're extra susceptible to the cold, and end up getting hypothermia. When you develop chills and become disoriented, Carlos insists on stopping at a clinic in the next town for treatment. After a couple of days, when you start to improve, you catch the flu, which puts a serious *damper* on your plans to finish the mission. The team can't afford to wait any longer for you to recover, so you are shipped home.

THE END

"Don't move!" you tell Jing. You slowly spread your arms out and stand tall, keeping eye contact with the jaguar. Inside your chest, your heart is pounding so hard you're sure the jaguar and Jing can hear it. Jing is frozen next to you. The jaguar is perfectly still, except you see its ear twitch. This is the scariest staring contest you've ever been in. But suddenly, the cat turns around and disappears into the trees.

"Oh my gosh," Jing says. "You did it!"

You feel faint for a moment, as what just happened hits you. But then, you just start walking in silence. After a couple hours, you reach a town where Jing is able to contact Carlos.

"Dan's doing better!" she says, handing you the phone.

You tell Carlos everything that's happened. A search party is sent for Nathan and Freddy, but they aren't found for days. Apparently, after Nathan started a fight and got an arrow through his shoulder, Freddy took him to his home village for treatment. Once he felt better, Nathan started filming Ashaninka life. Carlos is furious with the way they handled things—from start to finish.

All the wasted time and broken trust means the mission ends up falling apart. You're all sent home with nothing but the memories of what went wrong.

THE END

An hour passes and you're not any closer to camp. A few times, you and Jing think you've found the right path to take you back, but you just end up even more disoriented. As the minutes pass, you feel more and more anxious about what will happen if you don't get back to camp before dark.

"Look!" Jing points to the ground. "I think those are our tracks from earlier, when I spotted that beautiful parrot in that tree."

"I remember. Those should lead us straight back," you say. "Let's go!"

You and Jing take off in the direction of the tracks. As you're walking, Jing tells you a story from when she was a little kid.

"I lost my mom at a crowded market in Bangkok," she says. "It was so scary. Finally, I saw her coat and ran to her, but when I pulled on her hand, another lady turned around. I thought I'd never see her again, but somehow she found me, and we both cried."

"Well, I might cry when I finally see Carlos," you say, only half joking.

Then, suddenly, a short but intense tropical storm passes over you, drenching you both and—even worse—washing the tracks away.

"They're gone!" Jing cries, shaking her fists at the ground.

"I can't believe it!" you add. "This stinks! We don't have a portable GPS, or even a compass. What are we going to do?"

"I don't know. And it's going to get dark soon. Everyone at camp must be so worried," Jing says.

"Do you think they are looking for us?" you ask hopefully.

"Carlos has probably sent out some search parties. But who knows what direction they went in. And there hasn't been any sign of anyone yet."

"Well, I guess we can just keep walking," you say.

"Or we could stay here for the night," Jing suggests. "We could build a lean-to shelter out of branches and those big leaves where we can sleep for the night. It won't be very comfortable, but at least we'll have some protection from whatever comes out at night."

"But we don't have any food, and hardly any water. Who knows how long it will be before someone finds us if we stay here," you say.

At the same time, you are exhausted. Do you stay put, or keep trying to get back to camp?

IF YOU BUILD A SHELTER TO STAY IN THE JUNGLE FOR THE NIGHT, TURN TO PAGE 181.

IF YOU KEEP TRYING TO GET BACK TO CAMP, TURN TO PAGE 31.

THE JAGUAR IS ONLY A FEW PACES FROM YOU.

QUICK, LET'S GET OUT OF HERE!

ONE LUNGE AND YOU'LL BE HISTORY.

NO! LET'S LISTEN TO DAN!

DAN MAKES HIMSELF AS BIG AS POSSIBLE.

COPY ME!

YOU AND RANIA DO THE SAME.

YOU ARE IN A STARING CONTEST . . .

GRRRRRRRRRRRRRRRRRRRRRRR

You make your way back to camp and breathlessly tell the others about your close encounter with the jaguar.

"It's pretty uncommon to see one nowadays," Abadia says. "They are increasingly rare, even though the government banned hunting them."

"That was one of the scariest moments of my life," you say, feeling incredibly thankful that Dan was there to remind you what to do.

"You and Rania are lucky Dan was there to guide you," Carlos says, nodding approvingly as Rania tells him that it was Dan's quick thinking that helped you. "You wouldn't have been able to outrun the cat, so intimidating it was the right call."

The jaguar is the last of the major adventures you have on your trek. The final six weeks of your trip passes with only positive animal experiences, as you spot spider monkeys, macaws, sloths, and even a manatee for the team to study, photograph, and film.

By this point in the trek, you have started to feel really at home in the Amazon, and it seems like your body has gotten used to it too. Your feet have healed nicely with good care, and you notice that your skin doesn't even react to mosquito bites anymore.

As Freddy predicted, the biggest challenge of the last few weeks has been dealing with all the personalities of the team. As the end of the journey approaches and you're closer to getting home, everyone seems shorter on patience. And while you've been feeling happier in the jungle, others are getting really sick of it.

"I can't wait to get into a hotel with some nice dry sheets and a television," Dan whines at camp, stringing up his hammock for one of the last times.

"I want a long, hot shower. I'm tired of never feeling really clean and bathing in streams," Jing complains.

You have to admit, you could use a couch and a remote control for an afternoon. But you wonder what it'll be like to go back to life as usual after six months in the Amazon. How will it feel to be sitting in a classroom, studying biology in a book rather than staring at an amazing live plant or animal?

"I'm going to miss all this," you say to them. "Although I could sure go for a bowl of frosted cereal right now!"

The three of you discuss your favorite breakfast foods and debate the best kinds of pancakes.

After you complete the journey, you'll have a few days of rest with your family at a resort hotel, complete with soft beds, grand showers, televisions, and gourmet food—including cereal.

"All I know is that I'm going to be all over the buffet at the hotel we're going to. I heard it's really nice, and that it has a heated pool," Dan says.

You can't wait.

Four days later, you're staring out across the vast river from the bank. The river is now more like a sea in front of you, and you revel in the ability to see such a distance, after being enclosed in the tangled jungle all these months. Your eyes take a while to adjust, but the magnificent view makes you happier than ever.

You've almost arrived at the mouth of the Amazon and the conclusion of your expedition. For the dramatic finish of your journey, the team is going to travel by boat into the actual mouth of the river, where it empties into the Atlantic

Ocean. Camera crews and reporters from around the world are gathered to watch this historic moment.

The team is split into two-person teams to ride in the small boats. You're partnered with Nathan, who's good at handling boats. But as you look at the little boat, you can't help but notice the way the waves are rocking it. You wonder what it's going to feel like to get inside, and you feel your stomach turn.

The weather is windy and overcast and, looking at the dark clouds above, you're nervous that it might storm. As you look out into the water, it looks very threatening, so you decide to speak up.

"Nathan, I think we should wait for the water to calm down before we get into that boat," you say.

"Are you kidding? It's fine. The TV crews are waiting for us," he protests.

"Yeah, but look at those waves," you say. "I don't want to get tossed around in that. Our boat is tiny!"

"Don't worry, I can handle it," Nathan assures you with a wink. "Get in."

Even though Nathan's more experienced at handling a boat than you are, you're not sure what he can do to keep the little craft steady when the waves get bigger. And you imagine they *will* get bigger as you head out into the Atlantic Ocean.

But then again, Carlos and Jing have already left, and Dan and Rania are ready to head out after you. Wouldn't someone else have said something, especially Carlos, if the situation was really that unsafe?

You wonder if you're being overly cautious. Or are Nathan and the others just in a hurry to cross the finish line and get on TV, and too willing to take a risk?

Do you insist on waiting, or do you take a deep breath and step into the little boat so you don't miss your big moment?

IF YOU DECIDE TO GO AHEAD, TURN TO PAGE 185.

IF YOU INSIST ON WAITING, TURN TO PAGE 176.

You decide that the apple-like fruit looks too good to pass up. You pick the best-looking one, and after rubbing it against your shirt to clean off the little dirt you see, you take a large bite and chew slowly. Savoring the juice, you think about what it reminds you of, because it's not apple flavored. You take another bite and juices dribble down your chin. You'll take a bunch of these back to camp.

As you swallow the second bite, you start to feel strange. Suddenly your tongue swells in your mouth and your throat starts itching. You try to spit the remaining fruit out of your mouth, as you realize that you might be allergic to it—or *worse.* It could be poisonous. You feel cramps in your stomach and clutch it, doubling over. Next you start to vomit violently. You collapse to the ground, writhing in pain and waiting for the wave to pass. But the only thing that is going to *pass* is you, after several more increasingly painful hours, unless someone comes along to save you soon . . .

THE END

You start to run away from the peccaries, but the rumbling sound only gets louder. They're definitely headed your way!

"Quick! Climb a tree!" Dan shouts.

You look around frantically for a good tree to climb, but you don't see any branches low enough to grab hold of.

"I can't reach anything!" you yell, as you continue to run.

Suddenly, the stench of the peccaries overwhelms you. Now you know why they're sometimes called "skunk pigs." You can hear the chattering of their tusks hitting against each other, and you have a feeling of dread as you realize that you're about to be surrounded by the herd.

You turn around, and as far as you can see, the large, hairy pig-like animals are everywhere. You never wanted to be this close to an animal like *this*. You back up against a tree, putting your hands out in front of you, and try to look as non-threatening as possible. But that doesn't stop them.

You always wondered about people who chose to run with bulls in Spain—dashing through the narrow streets of Pamplona in front of wild, horned beasts—and you remember watching someone get gored on TV. Now you can sympathize, because you are gored by a dozen or more peccaries before Nathan and Carlos can come to your rescue with large sticks and scare away the herd.

Nathan was filming with his video camera, which was hanging around his neck, when Carlos shouted for his help, and he ended up accidentally recording you crying and yelling at the pigs to get away. Somehow the film ends up on the Internet, and after you are sent home for your injuries, you discover that you've become an overnight sensation as the "skunk pig kid." This isn't exactly the kind of fame you were hoping for. It really *stinks!*

THE END

You feel a lump in your throat when Carlos and Rania start to leave with Dan.

"Get better and come back soon," you say, giving Dan a fist bump. You sincerely hope that he'll be able to return and complete the mission. Despite his reckless decisions from time to time, you've grown really fond of Dan, and you have some nice memories of the time you spent together.

Jing wipes her eyes and gives Dan a hug. Everyone is sad to see him leave, and anxious about the future of the mission. Carlos gives Freddy instructions on where to take the team so you can still make progress toward your goal. If all goes well with Dan, Carlos and Rania will meet up with your team in a few days. If not, Carlos will send word about what will happen to the mission next.

That evening, you're sitting around the campfire with Nathan, Jing, and Freddy. The mood is glum, so to lighten it, Freddy starts to tell you about the legend of El Dorado.

"For the past five hundred years, people have been searching for a lost city of gold. The story is that when Spanish explorers reached South America, they heard about a tribe of people high up in the Andes mountains. This tribe had so much gold that their chief wore nothing but a layer of gold dust every day, and used to throw gold into the river to appease the gods."

"What happened to it?" Nathan asks.

"Well, people have been searching for it ever since. But no one has ever found it in all these years, and some people have even died trying. Now many people don't believe that it ever really existed. But my ancestors and I think it did."

"So do you know where El Dorado is?" you ask.

"I think I have an idea." Freddy smiles mysteriously.

"Well then, mate, what are we waiting for?" Nathan says. "Let's go find it!"

"Are you serious?" you and Jing both say together.

"Absolutely. Can you imagine what a fantastic film that would make? We can do this while the others figure out what's going on with Dan."

"I don't know," Freddy says. "I'm supposed to keep you on track."

"But do you *really* have an idea where El Dorado could be?" Nathan asks in an urgent tone.

"Yes," Freddy says, looking nervous but excited. "Not too far from here. And I've always wanted to find it."

"Then let's do it!" Nathan looks at you and Jing in turn. "Are you with me or not?"

What do you say?

IF YOU SAY, "YES, I'M IN," TURN TO PAGE 113.

IF YOU SAY, "NO, LET'S STICK TO THE MISSION," TURN TO PAGE 129.

You call your best friend back home and, after chatting and laughing for twenty minutes, everything seems better. Your conversation ends when your computer's battery goes dead, and you go to bed. Sadly, that's the last laugh you'll have for a while.

The next day, the team doesn't reach town before dark, and you can't recharge your battery. Things get worse when Carlos's handheld dies too. When it's time to make camp, the team has to guess about where will make a safe spot.

And . . . it's the wrong guess!

A flash flood wipes out half the camp, leaving you without enough supplies to continue.

THE END

YOU RUN FOR YOUR LIFE.

BUT THE JAGUAR IS HOT ON YOUR TAIL.

YOU REALIZE THAT YOU WON'T OUTRUN THE BIG CAT . . .

"Nathan, I'm not getting on that boat," you say.

"Come on, the cameras are waiting for us," he argues.

"I don't care. They can wait. Look!" you point ahead. The boat with Carlos and Jing is coming back toward you.

"The waves are rough out there!" Carlos shouts to you when you are within earshot. "We didn't want to risk anything."

You try hard not to give Nathan an I-told-you-so look.

"What about the news crews?" Nathan asks.

"They'll be there when we get there, don't worry. They've been waiting for us this long!" Carlos says with a laugh. "Besides, it adds suspense."

The team gathers around Carlos as the clouds darken. Within minutes, you're in a downpour with heavy winds. You take cover under tarpaulins that Dan and Nathan put up in a hurry.

"I'm glad we're not out in the water in that weather," Abadia says.

"Me, too," says Nathan, giving you a friendly jab in the shoulder. You can't be angry at him for being excited and fearless. That's who Nathan is, and it's partly why he's so successful at what he does.

"Shall we have some beans, for old time's sake?"

Nathan asks everyone as you huddle together.

"No, thanks!" you all reply in unison.

"I'm waiting for a burger," Dan says.

"Milkshakes are on me!" Rania offers.

"Listen, everyone," Carlos says. "I know we've had our ups and downs and some challenges along the way. But it's been an honor being your expedition leader. I've really enjoyed getting to know each of you over the past six months, and I will miss you all."

"Thank you, Carlos, for everything you taught us and for keeping us safe," Rania replies, her voice a little emotional.

"Three cheers for Carlos!" Nathan cries.

You all shout "hurray!" and give each other hugs. Your eyes start to fill up as you realize you don't know when you'll see your friends again after you say your final good-byes.

Finally the storm passes and the sun comes out.

"Look at that!" Jing says, pointing to the sky as she scrambles for her camera. It's a perfect rainbow. You can see every color in it, and it almost seems unreal. Then the rainbow's gone as quickly as it appeared.

You pile into your boats again and are glad to see that the water has calmed down considerably. And before you know it, your boat leaves the Amazon River and enters the Atlantic Ocean.

It's official! You've done it! Six months after your start date—surviving bee stings, peccaries, snakes, and jaguars, and navigating floods and friendships—you've made it to your destination. And it feels incredible!

You see the news crews set up on the beach, and as your boat docks, you realize that your life is never going to be the same again. Not only are you going to be on radio and television and online describing this experience, you're going to be listed in the *Guinness Book of World Records* as one of the youngest people ever to make the trip you did. That's pretty awesome!

A reporter asks you how you feel, and all you can say is, "This feels absolutely amazing!" And that reminds you of your first day of the trek. You look over at Nathan, and he winks at you, remembering. Dan and Jing give you thumbs-up. Rania and Carlos are beaming as they answer questions from reporters.

A few hours later, you're relaxing with your family after a joyous reunion in a luxurious hotel. Your stomach is full after a delicious meal, and you start to nod off on a cushy pillow. A moment later you're dreaming of your next adventure . . .

CONGRATULATIONS! YOU'VE ACHIEVED . . .

THE ULTIMATE SUCCESS

THE END!

You and Jing quickly line up a row of branches against a thicket of vines, creating a little tent-like shelter. Then you cover the gaps with large leaves. It's cramped and uncomfortable inside, and sleeping on the jungle floor makes your hammock seem like a luxury bed. But you feel a *little* safer hidden from some nocturnal predators. At least it's better than nothing.

As soon as it's light outside, you stir and wake up Jing.

"Let's get going," you say.

"Okay," she mumbles. "I'm so thirsty. Do you have any water left?"

You give her the last of the water you have with you, and you start to walk around, hoping to find camp, or for camp to find you. The tropical heat is fierce and soon you're sweating.

"We're out of water purification tablets," you tell Jing.

"We have to keep hydrated, or we could be in bigger trouble," she says.

"How about if we dig a hole near the river and let it fill up with water. We can filter it with my extra T-shirt," you suggest. The water won't be the cleanest, but it'll be something.

"I don't know," Jing says. "What if there are parasites or other germs in the water? That sounds risky to me."

Dehydration sounds riskier to you, and you are about to insist when Jing suddenly points to the ground.

"Look! Those are peccary tracks. We know peccaries are always looking for fruit. If we follow the tracks, I'm sure we'll find a fruit tree, and we can replenish with some fruit juices."

Mmm. Fruit juice sounds delicious right now. Not only are you thirsty, but you haven't eaten in a long time, and the idea of a ripe guava or papaya makes your stomach gurgle.

At the same time, the peccary tracks could be a wild goose—or *pig*—chase. What if they don't lead to anything? At least your idea guarantees water, even if it's a little dirty.

IF YOU DIG THE HOLE AND DRINK THE FILTERED WATER, TURN TO PAGE 58.

IF YOU FOLLOW THE PECCARY TRACKS, TURN TO PAGE 56.

You hurry toward the Ticuna boy to see what he is trying to say to you. As you get closer, you see him start to gesture more frantically, and then you see horror register on his face. Suddenly, you realize why. There's a giant pit viper coiled in a tree branch right at the level of your head. The poisonous snake's tan-and-dark-brown body blended in so well with the tree branch it's sitting on that you hadn't noticed it at all. And you didn't remember that the word "*culebra*" means "snake" in Spanish. The Ticuna boy was trying to prevent you from coming any closer!

You freeze in your tracks, but the viper is poised to strike. You've come too near, and you were moving too fast, so it considers you a threat. The next thing you know, you see an outstretched snake mouth with pointed fangs heading toward you. Everything feels like it's happening in slow motion, but you can't do anything to stop it . . . or get away. You cover your face with your arm and feel the fangs sink into your skin.

The pain of the bite is excruciating, and unlike anything you've ever experienced before. But that's just the beginning. You look at your arm and try to remember everything you know about venom and how it spreads through the body. Trying to suck the poison out with your mouth won't help. Instead, you try to stay calm and keep the bitten area below your heart. Now you just have to try to get back to camp, and to Rania, so she can administer some anti-venom before it's too late. You walk toward the Ticuna boy saying, "Help me, please!" and then . . . pass out. Unfortunately, there's nothing he— or anyone else—can do to save you. There's just not enough time.

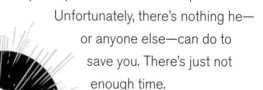

THE END

Before you get in the boat, you hesitate for a moment, looking out again at the rough waters ahead of you.

"Come on! We're wasting time," Nathan says.

"Are you sure you don't want to wait?" you ask. "Aren't you a little worried about going out there?"

"Nah, it'll be fine! Carlos and Jing are already out there and are going to wonder where we are. And Rania and Dan are going to come right behind us. Let's go!"

You give in and carefully step into the boat. This is a lot smaller than the other boats you've been traveling in, and you're surprised by how much it rocks and how you feel every wave. Even though you don't have that far to travel, you hope you can stomach the journey without losing your lunch.

"You're not going to get seasick on me, are you?" Nathan asks, looking at you with an amused expression.

"I'll be okay," you say, swallowing hard. "Let's get this over with."

You push away from the shore.

"I love the water. I guess it's a big part of me, since I grew up on an island," Nathan says. Can you believe we're almost at the Atlantic?"

You are fully submerged in the chilly water, which is rushing over your head. Kicking your feet, you finally come up gasping for air.

"Grab this rope!" you hear Nathan shouting. He's managed to climb back into the boat, and he's throwing you a line.

You try to reach for the rope, but it keeps moving away from you. As the waves crash over your head, you are gulping down water.

Trying desperately to keep above water, you try to swim back to the boat. But the current is so strong, it tosses you around like a rubber ducky in a whirlpool. You're not making any progress, and the boat is slowly moving farther and farther away from you. You look back and forth between the boat and the shore and decide to try to get back to land instead. But your muscles are burning from the effort of swimming and your lungs are hurting.

"Don't stop!" Nathan shouts. "Keep moving!"

You try to keep moving, but you're just so tired. The waves are pulling you down and you don't have anything left in you to fight against them. You close your eyes and surrender to the waves, hoping the water will wash you to a safe place . . .

THE END

AMAZON EXPEDITION FILE

Olá amigos!

I put together this information for you to read before the trip. It's important stuff, so make sure you know it all. I don't want anyone losing a fingertip to a piranha! I look forward to meeting all of you. And keep up your training hikes!

- Carlos

FROM SOURCE TO MOUTH: OUR ROUTE

Length of trip: About six months
Distance: More than 4,000 miles (6,437 km)

The river has dangerous rapids here, so we can't use our boats.

Nevado Mismi: 18,363 feet (5,597 meters)

We'll need to watch the waves here as they can get very big If we don't time our crossing right, our small boats could get flipped over.

1 This is the source of the Amazon, a spring on the slope of Mt. Nevado Mismi.

After we climb to the spring, we descend and trek through mossy, treeless terrain for about three weeks.

2 Here it is safe to use our boats. We will ride for a week to the jungle.

3 Here we enter the jungle. We'll walk and use our inflatable rafts.

4 Some of the native people we will meet in this remote area will have never seen a foreigner before, and they might be afraid of us, or even hostile.

5 This is Manaus, a big city in the middle of the rain forest. We'll stop here for supplies.

Here the Negro River and the muddy Solimões River come together to form the Amazon River.

6 The local people in this region usually have seen foreigners before, as there is much more tourism here. They typically speak both Portuguese and their native language.

7 Our journey ends with a boat ride into the Atlantic.

ANIMALS
OF THE AMAZON

And how NOT to get bitten, poisoned, or gored

The Amazon rain forest covers almost half of South America. It's the biggest rain forest on the planet, and it's the home of the longest and largest river in the world, the Amazon River. It's also home to countless species of plants, insects, and animals. Here's a little introduction to a few jungle residents you just might run into on the trip.

Poison Dart Frog

These colorful little frogs are beautiful—and deadly.

Don't touch these frogs. Their skin secretes a powerful poison that can kill you if it comes into contact with an open wound.

Jaguar

These big cats, which are either spotted or all black, hunt a huge range of prey, including peccaries, tapir, sloths, monkeys, reptiles, and fish.

Do face the jaguar with your arms spread out, making yourself look as big and threatening as possible. Make loud noises. Hopefully the jaguar will just slink off into the jungle.

Don't turn away or run. This will make the jaguar want to chase you down—and you won't outrun it!

Anaconda

Anacondas aren't poisonous snakes—they kill their prey by wrapping themselves around the animal and squeezing ("constricting") it to death.

Don't worry about an anaconda giving you the squeeze. This is very unlikely—they don't see you as prey.

Do avoid them when walking or swimming near a riverbank. They bite, and the bite can make a nasty wound.

Peccary

These wild pig-like animals roam the Amazon in herds. Beware—there can be as many as a hundred in a herd, and they can trample you and gore you with their tusks.

Do make a loud, scary sound like "whoo! whoo!" when you hear them in the distance. This should scare them away.

Caiman

There are four different species of these Amazonian reptiles, the largest of which, the black caiman, grows up to 14 feet (4.3 meters) long!

Do avoid their nests, which are mounds of grass, twigs, and mud.

Don't splash in the water near their nests (or where there's any sign of them)—they may mistake you for prey.

INSECTS & SPIDERS
OF THE AMAZON

And how to avoid stings, bites, and larvae growing under your skin!

The Amazon rain forest is home to an incredible range of insects—some estimates suggest that more than 30 million different species live there! Here's a short introduction to a few you'll want to know about.

Mosquitoes

There's no avoiding these jungle pests. Repellent gets washed off by sweat and water.

Do apply repellent often and take anti-malaria medicine.

Do sleep under a mosquito net.

Do sit near a campfire—"mozzies" don't like smoke.

Tarantulas

These hairy spiders live in holes in the ground and can grow as big as a dinner plate in the Amazon.

Don't worry about them—they aren't likely to bite you. They're most interested in eating insects. And even if you do get bitten, it's no worse than a bee sting.

Bees and Wasps

Bees and wasps make their nests under leaves and get very angry when you slice their home with a machete on your way past. Here's what to do if you get swarmed.

Do run and dive face-first on the ground.

Do cover your mouth so they can't sting inside it.

Don't throw off your backpack. It will prevent your back from being stung.

Botflies

A botfly larva can crawl under your skin and grow there! The larva creates a painful red mound and eventually wriggles out.

Don't dig at the mound, because you could end up with a serious infection.

Do put tape over the hole in the center of the mound. This is the larva's airhole. Without an air supply, the larva dies, and then it can be carefully squeezed out of the hole.

Tarantula Hawk Wasps

This giant wasp is more interested in tarantulas—which it kills to feed its young—than it is in you. But if it does sting you, the pain is severe!

Don't swat at it. It is only aggressive toward humans if you're aggressive first.

THE PEOPLE
OF AMAZONIA

Your Amazon adventure will bring you into contact with a wide range of people. You'll meet some who live in small towns and big cities, and you'll also find small tribes with little or no contact with the outside world. Some of these people will welcome outsiders, but others won't, fearing that foreigners will bring disease and destruction.

Near Manaus, Brazil

Say it like a Local

Amazon natives will speak their own tribal language and sometimes also Spanish or Portuguese. It pays to know some of each!

	Spanish (Peru)	Portuguese (Brazil)
Hello	Hola (OH-la)	Olá (OH-la)
Thank you	Gracias (GRAH-see-us)	Guys: Obrigado (oh-bree-GAH-doh) Girls: Obrigada (oh-bree-GAH-dah)
Let's go!	Vamos (VAH-mos)	Bora la! (BOR-a-la)
Be careful!	Cuidado! (kwee-DAH-doh)	Cuidadoso! (kew-dah-DOH-soh)
Snake	Culebra (ku-LAY-bra)	Cobra (KOH-bra)
Fish	Pescado (pes-CAH-doh)	Peixe (PESH-ay)

YOUR PACKING LIST

Before you know it, it'll be time to pack! Here's what you'll need to carry.

Your guides will handle the navigation equipment and most of the medical and cooking supplies.

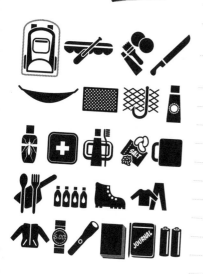

Backpack with waterproof liner

Inflatable one-person raft and paddles

Raft-patching kit

Machete (18 inches [46 cm])

Hammock

Mosquito net

Fishing kit (hooks, wire leads, reel, net)

Sunscreen

Mosquito repellent

Medicine kit

Basic toiletries
(soap, toothbrush, toothpaste)

Your share of food
(rice, beans, salt and spice packets)

Mug

Pot and utensils

4 water bottles (1-liter size)

Hiking clothing and boots

Camp clothing and shoes

Waterproof jacket

Waterproof watch with light and alarm

Flashlight

Book to read

Journal and pen

Your share of spare batteries

How to Survive Venomous Snakes

Venomous snakes in the Amazon fall into two categories—pit vipers and coral snakes. Fortunately, snake bites are rare, and even if you do get bitten, the snake won't always inject its venom. But still, it's important to follow these precautions.

1 ### Watch the trees

Most of the snakes you'll encounter will be vipers hanging out in trees, often right at eye level. Because vipers are very good at camouflage, you could get very close before you notice them. If you *do* find yourself eye-to-eye with a viper, avoid making a sudden move, which might encourage the snake to strike. Just slowly back away.

2 ### Walk with a native

People who grew up in the jungle are much better at spotting snakes than foreigners are. Follow their lead.

3 Kick before you pick

Snakes often hide out under logs on the forest floor, and bites can happen while campers are collecting firewood. So, before picking up a log, give it a good kick. This will startle the snake, and it will probably slither off, looking for a new place to hide. If you reach with your hand first, the snake may bite your finger.

4 Carry anti-venom

Your guide will carry anti-venom—enough to give you 48 hours to get to a hospital. Venom can kill very quickly, so get the anti-venom shot immediately. Signs of "envenomation" (a venom-loaded bite) include swelling or numbness at the site, as well as nausea and weakness.

Red on Black, Venom Lack?

Coral snakes got their name because explorers thought they looked like the colorful coral found in tropical seas. They have bands—usually some combination of red, yellow, and black.

There are coral snakes in North America, too, but not all of them are venomous. To remember which ones have venom, people say, "Red on yellow, kill a fellow. Red on black, venom lack." However, this rhyme does not work in the Amazon. There, a venomous coral snake may have any pattern of bands. Fortunately, coral snakes rarely bite humans—their mouths are too small to get a good grip on anything much larger than a finger or toe.

How to Fish for Piranhas

Despite their scary reputation, piranhas probably won't bother you while you're swimming. You're more likely to run into trouble after you've fished one out of the river. That's right—piranhas are easy to catch, so you'll often be eating *them* for dinner. But how do you catch a fish with razor-sharp teeth? Very carefully!

1 Use a wire leader

Piranhas can bite the hook right off the line. So, use a wire leader—a 4-inch (10-cm) wire between the hook and the line.

2 Don't let your catch hang out in the net

You can also catch piranhas with regular fishing nets. Just don't leave the net in the water for long, as other piranhas will come and eat the ones that are trapped!

3 Handle with care!

Unless you want to lose a fingertip, only grab a piranha from behind the gills. And if you're fishing in a raft, keep your catch contained. Loose piranhas could bite your toes!

How to Avoid Dehydration

It's so hot in the Amazon, you'll be losing lots of fluid through sweat. Here's how to make sure you don't run low on H_2O.

1 Drink about 3 to 4 liters of water per day

Drink often—don't wait until you feel thirsty. If your urine is dark yellow and you're not peeing much, you're in trouble. Drink more!

2 Eat plenty of food—with salt

Make sure to eat a lot of food, because your body will be losing essential minerals called *electrolytes* as you sweat. A key electrolyte is sodium, so make sure to add salt to your food.

Electric Eels!

Electric eels are not really eels—they're relatives of catfish that look like eels. They can deliver a big enough shock to knock a person unconscious, so be very careful, because people can drown if they fall in the water after the jolt. If this happens, pull the victim out of the water without getting in yourself, as an eel can linger nearby and very easily shock you, too.

How to Set Up Camp in the Jungle

Every night for the five months we're in the jungle, you'll have to find a spot to hang your hammock. Here's how to do it right.

1 **Look up**

Check the trees above you for deadwood that could fall on you.

deadwood

2 **Look for signs of high water**

When the river has recently flooded, there will be residue (scum) on the leaves and a high-water mark (a line of scum) on the trees. Avoid camping anywhere you see these signs.

3 **Get help from an "eye in the sky"**

Satellite images can help you spot areas that are likely to flood.

Trees

Trees

Muddy, streaky areas indicate recent flooding.

More Jungle Survival Tips

Food: Don't eat any fruit or nut from the jungle without checking with a guide, who will use this test:

- Put a bit on the skin and check for a reaction.
- Put a bit on the tongue and wait a few minutes.
- If there's no reaction, eat a tiny portion and wait an hour. If nothing happens, it's probably safe.

Water: Never drink water directly from the river—there are parasites in the water that'll make you sick. Use water purification tablets always. If you're lost and don't have any:

- Create a makeshift filter by digging a hole in the sand on the riverbank, about 1 foot (31 cm) deep.
- The hole will fill with water from below, passing through sand that will filter out some impurities.
- Stretch a clean T-shirt over your water bottle and pour the water through it to filter out even more "nasties."

Clothing: Wear light, loose clothes in the jungle, and keep a warm, waterproof jacket for boat trips on the river. It's windy out there, and if you're wet, you can get quite a chill.

Shelter: Always sleep under a net to avoid bites from mosquitoes, which carry malaria. A net (or any shelter) will also protect you from vampire bats!

Health: Open wounds can quickly get infected in the hot and wet jungle. If a wound just won't heal, you may need antibiotics. Don't wait too long—the infection could spread.

Safety: If a tree falls toward you, don't run directly away from it. Trees are tall, so you won't outrun the full length of the trunk. Run to either side.

ABOUT THE CONTRIBUTORS

AUTHORS

Hena Khan hopes to visit the Amazon rain forest someday, and now that she has written this Ultimate Adventure, she'll be prepared! She lives in Rockville, Maryland, with her husband and two sons.

David Borgenicht is the co-author of all the books in the "Worst-Case Scenario" series. He lives in Philadelphia.

CONSULTANT

Ed Stafford became the first person ever to walk the entire length of the Amazon River on August 9, 2010. His journey took 860 days and was more than 4,000 miles (6,437 km) long. He tells the story in his book, *Walking the Amazon.* He lives in London, England.

ILLUSTRATOR

Yancey Labat got his start with Marvel Comics and has since been illustrating children's books. He lives in New York.